SKELMERSDALE

FICTION RESERVE STOCK LL60

AUTHOR

BRINK, HANS M. vanden

CLASS

AF

TITLE

ON THE WATER

D0279395

On the Water

On the Water

H. M. VAN DEN BRINK

Translated from the Dutch
by Paul Vincent

faber and faber

First published in the Netherlands in 1998
by J. M. Meulenhoff
First published in Great Britain in 2001
by Faber and Faber Limited
3 Queen Square London WC1N 3AU

Typeset by Faber and Faber Ltd
Printed in Italy

© H. M. van den Brink, 1998
This translation © Paul Vincent, 2001

Paul Vincent is hereby identified as translator
of this work in accordance with Section 77 of the
Copyright, Designs and Patents Act 1988

Publication of this work has been made possible
with financial support from the Foundation for the
Production and Translation of Dutch Literature

A CIP record for this book
is available from the British Library

ISBN 0–571–20152–0

2 4 6 8 10 9 7 5 3

For Pieter

I

I last heard the planes half an hour ago. They crossed the river diagonally at high altitude and then their deep roar faded away to the east. Now it is quiet again, except for the noises that go with a winter's night by the water's edge. Restless wind. Waves lapping the posts of the jetty. No birds. No sudden cries anywhere. There is, though, somewhere behind me on the quay, the occasional rattle of a window that isn't properly closed. I'm standing alone on the furthest jetty, its wood black with moisture and slippery as glass, and am looking intently at the water. On the far bank of the river lies the city, windows blacked out, aimless tram rails, treeless streets. I am looking at the far bank but can scarcely see it any longer.

For a moment I imagined what it would be like to fly east in the planes. I pictured what it was like in the confined space of the cockpit, with men in leather jackets doing their work silently. A single gesture is enough for them to understand each other. There is only the light of a couple of monitor lamps, green and blue. An illuminated dial. Perhaps the glow of a cigarette. Then I thought of the vast space below the belly of the plane, the keel seeking its way through the thin air, with nothing to hang on to, no support, and I began to feel dizzy. I thought of the distance between the men and their target and of what slid beneath them meanwhile, small and invisible: the polders, the heath and the woods, the farms with their steep roofs, groups of houses huddling together against the cold in the villages, the towns with their factories and around them the grey streets where at this moment people everywhere are sitting together with the same black paper over the windows. I thought of the lakes, the canals large and small, the ditches and the rivers. I thought especially of the water because water, silvery, is the first to wake when day breaks and life begins anew.

Across the river lies the city. I can't see it, but it's as if I can feel how heavily and anxiously it is breathing. Like some great animal that has been hibernating for too long, and stinking, far too thin, wonders if it will ever wake up. I can scarcely see even the bridge from here, the bridge with its elegant lamps that links the suburbs and the stately houses on the embankment behind me. I shiver in my raincoat. I sit down. I close my eyes. Sleet strikes my face.

But when I lean back and stretch out I suddenly feel the wood warm down my spine and against the backs of my legs once more, as if the warmth had been waiting there for me all those years. And then it is summer again and above me I see an almost cloudless, brilliant blue sky, a dome of air stretched tautly across the river, the city and the country. All day long the sun has warmed the planks of the jetty until they are cooked through, light grey, almost white, and red hot. In a second the sun also dries my sweaty face, leaving only salt, which feels grainy on my skin.

The jetty is actually a raft that is attached by metal rings to a number of posts alongside the boathouse, so that it can move up and down as the level of the river rises and falls. It slowly sways in time with the afternoon waves, almost imperceptibly, except when, like me, you lie back languidly and float away on your exhaustion and no longer know where your body ends and where the wood, the water and the sky begin. In the distance I hear David calling.

I don't answer.

I close my eyes.

When I open them, he has come up behind me. I look up along his legs, which are powerful and covered in dark-brown hair; I see that he has taken his shirt off and put it over his shoulders.

'Done in?'

I can't see his face properly, but I know the kind of look he's giving me. Sarcastic. Friendly and sarcastic. That's how he always looks. He has the face and body of someone who at birth was given not just a life, but the whole world in his lap. That's why he approaches us, the others, so calmly, with his friendly irony.

'Shattered? Too much for you?'

I say nothing and do not accept the hand that is offered to help me up. I'm not an invalid, far from it. I roll on to my side and in a rapid, supple movement stand up beside him. When I'm standing I'm as tall as he is. Not as powerfully built. Not as calm. But just as tall.

Now I can see that he is tired too. Sweat is still streaming from under his black curls, along his nose, into his mouth. He grimaces and wipes it away with his rolled-up shirt. For the first time I dare to think that he is not just my partner, but more than that, perhaps a friend. We have trained hard. Under the fierce sun, under the clear sky, we have rowed as fast as we could along the river. A little way down the pontoon is the empty boat, its brass gates flashing, the oars crossed. We lift the boat out of the water. We wipe the cedarwood shell with a cloth to dry it, take it inside and fetch the oars. And then, as we walk together to the shed, each of us carrying an oar, David puts his hand on my shoulder for a moment. Not just friendly, but like a real friend. Not sarcastic, but serious. I'm so tired. I squeeze the hard wood of the oar and feel my muscles flex one last time. A wave of deep happiness sweeps through my hands, my arms, my shoulders, my chest and my legs. I am tired and happy.

Happiness? You shouldn't talk about it. One word too many and it becomes ridiculous. Two words and it's vanished, gone. And yet it doesn't feel fragile, the happiness of this summer. You can take hold of it and lay your head on it. I hold it in my hand for hours and it doesn't go away.

And now too I am holding on to that summer, not just in my thoughts, but with my whole body, from my numb fingers down to my toes. That summer when the river was ours, and so was the boathouse, the city, the meadows and the reeds at the water's edge. Happiness only exists when you can touch it and I held it, I'm still holding it, that summer of 1939, now, here, tonight. I hear the soft chatter of the water and deep in my bones I can still feel the warmth of the planks of the pontoon.

My first memory of the river consists mainly of light and

space. I see myself and my father walking through the streets of our neighbourhood, along Topaz Street, past the square with the public baths and then into the wide Emerald Street, which did not lead to another street but issued on to the wide avenue along the river and hence into a sea of sunlight where trees rustled and flags flapped and crowds of people were abroad and where noise did not fill the space but fanned out in all directions, over the water and up into the sky.

I must have been about two or three, not much older, because I was sitting on my father's shoulders and my father is small and delicate and not strong. I think there was a regatta or some other form of water festivity to which he had taken me, because in my memory the river is a carpet of silver wavelets with countless boats of all shapes and sizes.

Since then I have been to many of those festive days and although they sometimes say the first impression is always the strongest, I am not aware that my joy at such river festivities has diminished. It was more like love at first sight, which then grew ever deeper and more intense. Later, I loved it when on holidays the river filled with pleasure craft, cruisers, rowing boats, punts, scows and sailboats, flat-bottomed vegetable barges of wood and iron, elegant clinker-built wherries, tugs, and whatever else can float and sail, all decked out and packed with cheerful people laughing and shouting about nothing, just because the sun is shining and they can stand and sit without any firm base underfoot, for the sheer joy of a beautiful, useless day on the river. I also got to know the river in empty moments, under scudding clouds, with waves that batter each other and make even the sturdiest ship feel alone and vulnerable; in the winter, just before the water turns to ice; in the autumn; in the treacherous spring; in summer rain when the water is suddenly lashed out of its indolence and is pockmarked by an unexpected downpour at the end of the day – and I grew to love all those faces. The river taught me the meaning of movement and taught me that movement is life. Does that sound exaggerated? Perhaps it is. But that's what I feel, and I can't help it.

On that first day when I consciously saw the water I must already have felt some of its special power. Or perhaps I made that day into the first time because I now know the end of the story. Be that as it may, besides the colours and the shimmering I remember one image in particular that made an indelible impression on me.

The afternoon was drawing to a close, it had already got quieter on the river and in the surrounding streets. We had walked along the quayside and climbed up the steps of the bridge with the cast-iron lamps, the bridge which grandly and elegantly links the mansions on the quiet bank of the river with the city. We stopped half-way across the bridge. My father lifted me off his shoulders and let me lean over the railing and look down. Seen from as close up as this, the water was not silver but greyish blue and green. At the very moment that I leaned right over and my father tried to hold me back by my armpits, a pointed brass tip shot into view from under the arch of the bridge, followed by an almost equally slender bow covered with silvery-white material. There was no time to recover from that first astonishment,

6

because the canvas was followed by the first, second, third of eight men in all who were drawn out from under the bridge like a string of pearls, or rather who drew themselves out, riding and gliding, jack-knifing and reaching forwards to the left and right as they engaged the water with their long oars, pushing it away from them and letting go of it again, eight men in white shirts in perfect rhythm, followed by a small cox in a blue jacket holding a brass megaphone, like the dot under a long exclamation mark. It was over in a few seconds, but for as long as I could I stared after the rowers, and not just the rowers, but also the trail that they were pulling with them from under the bridge, a trail of lines and whirlpools, where the oars had hit the water hard, like footprints that the moment they were made immediately started erasing themselves, after first slowly merging into one another.

I don't know what made the greatest impression on me at that moment, the supple way the men moved together or the movement they caused in the river.

I only know that I held my breath. Because when I recall it, I still do.

My father was small and delicate and not strong. It did not take me long to recognize this. This realization, though, had nothing to do with muscular strength. Every child has confidence in its father's power as long as he is able to stand between it and the world. But even before I could think about such things, let alone talk about them, I must have sensed that my father could only just about hold his own in that world. I could see that from the timid way he left the house every morning in the dark-grey uniform of the tram company – my father must have been the only man in the world who did not derive power and authority from wearing a uniform, but instead projected even more anxiety and helplessness, as if people could now see all the more clearly that he wore his clothes like a shield. And it also had something to do with the way in which he came back home again every evening, like an animal that is glad to have reached its lair but still can scarcely believe it is safe. And that was how my mother treated him. Softly mumbling and moaning, she fluttered round the chair into which he had flopped. She poured him a cup of coffee or chicory, she loosened his collar, she lugged in a basin of water for his bunion-covered feet.

I never despised my father for what he was, indeed I am certain I loved him. First, because there was a time, a short time, when he really could lift me up and carry me around outside on his shoulders, and later because I saw that he had to summon up so much courage to keep going outside that there was really nothing left for his wife and child. I understood from an early age that I was left to my own devices. It made me a quiet, introverted boy who made up his own games among the furniture and fabrics of the flat and whose only choice was to triumph over or be beaten by himself. Later, a serious and dutiful schoolboy, who because of his inability to get in the last word was sometimes regarded by others as sneaky. The only child between two parents who had their hands full with themselves in a dark, narrow house.

For my parents, that house with its weird bays and its windows scarcely bigger than shooting slits must have been a dream come true. They were the first occupants, the cement was not dry in the mortar courses when they followed their simple furniture up the stairs. It was not the new street that was important to them, not the neighbourhood and certainly not the neighbours, who were all new and strangers to each other, but who from day one were busy saying hello, arranging meetings, paying visits, telling stories, doing mutual favours, organizing their lives to make them congenial and cheerful and worthwhile. As far as they could, my parents withdrew from all social intercourse. It wasn't people, it was the house itself from which they expected security and happiness, the roof, the ceilings, the walls, bricks and mortar. I'm quite sure they entered it that first time with the firm intention of becoming one with every cranny and skirting board, so that it would be not only socially, but biologically impossible ever to tear them away. For them it was an advantage that the house was dark and poky, because its function was to be as little as possible like the rest of the world.

Our neighbourhood had been planned in the Depression by the city's strong men, patriarchs with a social conscience who saw it as their sacred duty to give the population four walls and a roof over their heads. But only in theory did they recognize people's right to accommodation according to their own requirements and taste. Or else they would have given us residents light, space and big windows instead of subjecting us to a geometrically pure street plan, a succession of squares, shops, bathhouses and doorways which one could traverse in only one direction and a house

9

design that was so compelling that not so much as a chair, let alone a table or a settee, could be placed in a spot which the powers-that-be considered socially irresponsible.

The streets were distinguished solely by the house fronts. Some undulated and finished up in sharp right angles, others started out straight but converged in series of round towers, crowned with battlements, as if the Middle Ages had paid a flying visit. The bricks had been laid in the strangest shapes to create a fascinating pattern of lines and shapes, not for the benefit of the individual houses or their residents, but as a constituent part and embellishment of the whole, the street, the neighbourhood aesthetics. Roof tiles, windowframes, gutters, staircases, even the house numbers seemed intended in the first instance as ornaments. They were not ours and never would be; we were simply allowed to live behind them.

My parents were the ideal residents for this new neighbourhood. Citizens who were sincerely happy with what little the authorities granted them. Faceless people, the extras on the architectural drawings that were admired at home and abroad. Obedient children of those well-intentioned patriarchs, children who, once put in their place, would never utter a word of complaint and in gratitude would not move any more than was absolutely necessary and required.

The countless times I heard my parents say that it was a great blessing that my father had not only been able to find a house, but had found a house close to his job. He worked for the municipal transport company, in the big tram depot, which exits by means of a wide row of doors on to the river bank. The gleaming rails follow the course of the water for a moment then turn off in various directions, to the city centre where the big shopping streets are, the warehouses and the Royal Palace, to the docks, to the station, to other suburbs which did not stop at the waterfront like ours but got bogged down in the meadows, with their gardens, animals and water slurry. My father never saw any of those places, I suspect, and I'm sure he was never curious about them. His job was in the depot, he looked after the trams that were at a standstill, after the maintenance of pipes and wheels, after the cleaning of floors and seats. The depot is often quiet and dark also. It was a home away from home for him.

There is another memory from my childhood that concerns the river. It was a hot, boiling-hot summer's day. I was five or six. Sand had been dumped for the construction of the new bridge. The new bridge belonged to our neighbourhood: built in the style of our streets, and brazenly equipped with tram rails, modern lamps and wiring, it was to disrupt the quiet dignity of the other bank. I can still see the floating cranes, the piles and the partitions in the water. And I can see the sand. There was so much that a temporary golden-white beach was created in the middle of town, a beach that began a little below the shore and undulated seductively towards the coolness of the river.

It must have been the heat that drove my mother out of the house. She wasn't someone who would set out on a walk on a weekday for no good reason. And it must also have been the heat that made her walk to the little beach.

But perhaps it was me too who, small as I was, and craftily making use of her awkwardness, followed my penchant for water and directed her steps. She wore a dress of uncomfortable rayon-silk and a white pudding-basin hat with a ribbon. The summer wardrobe. As I walked beside her I could smell her sad, sweaty aroma, and the closer we got to the river and the beach, the more I had the feeling that she was losing her power over me, that she couldn't stop me, that now I really was deciding what was going to happen. She stopped on the bank as I ran down. I heard a final warning but paid no attention to it and her voice was lost almost immediately in the babble of voices around me. Scores of children, some in swimming costumes but most in vests and underpants, were splashing about in the water and teeming over the beach. Laughing faces, skinny legs, tummies, shoulders, white and pink and red and brown skin – and over all that a shower of water droplets and sunbeams, a bright fog of fun. I took a deep breath. Then I took my shoes off. And my socks. I left them behind on the sand, and in my short trousers and cotton shirt I walked slowly towards the water. At that moment, in my memory, all the noise stops for a moment. No screaming and howling children, no calling mother. A solemn moment. In a shaft of silence I entered the water. A little John the Baptist, although the Saviour was a long way off yet.

When the waves reached my knees I stopped. Was it then that I realized I was the only fully dressed child among all those other, half-naked water creatures? I don't know. All I know is that I stared at my legs and saw how puny and white they were and felt how wonderful the dark water was that enclosed my shins like a vase.

I stood there until the noise came back and then I unbuttoned my shirt, took off my vest, and smacked the water with one hand. I looked around me at the other children and smiled cheerfully at them, although none of them were paying any attention to me. A barge came past and launched a set of rollers towards the beach, to general acclaim. The water splashed against my skinny chest and I shivered with joy. With my hand I stroked my ribs, which I could feel one by one. I felt my soft little belly and realized I had goose pimples, but not from the cold. My clean short trousers were darkened by the waves. I turned round.

On the bank my mother was gesticulating wildly, but not *too* wildly, because she didn't want to make a scene. She was only worried about me. I pretended not to see her for a moment. I threw my clothes down on dry land and ran along the water's edge. I plunged my arms into the water, splashed at no one in particular, felt the sun and the water together. It was not the grandness of the river that enchanted me this time, but precisely the tangibility, the closeness of the water. You could touch it, it mixed with sand and turned into mud, with air and became rain, you could feel it between your fingers and, although it was gone again in an instant, you had at least made it move.

I looked at the bank again and saw my mother still signalling for me to come back. Why didn't she come to me? Why didn't she come and get me? The rayon dress would darken at the hem, the pudding-basin hat would float on the waves. I knew it was impossible. I took a couple of wild steps towards the middle of the river, then I went back like a good boy. Suddenly, a strange feeling in my right foot.

I must have stepped on a nail. When I lifted up my foot and turned it over I saw a delta of bright red blood spreading very fast across the pale sole. It didn't hurt. I dipped my foot in the water again and watched in fascination as the scene repeated itself. Limping, shoes in hand and putting my clothes back on as I walked, I returned to the shore. My mother had got even hotter than just before. I could smell that. She pulled me to her, whimpering softly, and pushed me away again to look at the wound. I heard her gasping for breath and then she pulled me close again, with my nose in the artificial silk, and in that way tried to drag me along with her, still only half-dressed, across the road and home as quickly as possible. In her panic she paid no attention to the traffic. I felt the rough heat of the cobbles on my bare feet and heard the furious ringing of the tram. The carriages grazed past us. My mother stood stock-still, sobbing and shivering, and then came to her senses. On the traffic island she put my socks and shoes on. Probably she shot a worried look in the direction of the tram depot, an apologetic look, because that's where my father was. With her hand on the scruff of my neck, she pushed me towards our house, her shapeless belly occasionally bumping into me. I couldn't imagine that I had ever come out of there and I knew that I had nothing more to do with it. She probably never told my father about our visit to the beach and of her panicky failure. Nor did we go near there again that summer. I do remember that many months later there was satisfied talk at home about the building work in the neighbourhood being finished. Everything was sealed. The last brick had been laid. Now there would be peace for ever.

I don't know what my father makes of it, the whole world apparently coming to a standstill. He likes stillness in general, but not a disruption of the normal course of events. I think he was only satisfied when all the trams had driven into the sheds, been cleaned and checked, and the doors shut. He probably regarded their driving round the city at large, ringing, accelerating, braking abruptly, weaving their way through the seething throng, with all those strange people getting on and off, as a necessary evil. For the last few months there have been no more trams running in the city. The rails are being taken up and where they are still down their surface is not shiny but dull and black. Sleepers and blocks have been taken up by heads of families looking for fuel. But the big sheds too are virtually empty, the best carriages and trams have been confiscated and transported to the east to be put to work in the bombed cities. Yet I think my father still goes out every morning and walks the few hundred metres to the depot to supervise and maintain the paltry remnants of his vehicle fleet. I imagine him, with a pullover under his uniform, polishing cloth and notepad in hand, doing his rounds and his footsteps forlornly echoing in the dim sheds.

I would never do anything like that. Wasted effort, useless ritual. At least, that's what I felt till tonight. But perhaps I'm now discovering a slight similarity between the two totally different people I thought we were. Because why have I come here? Behind me is what's left of the boathouse. The top section, with the club and the terraces, has been more or less completely demolished, the sheds in which the boats were kept are still standing. I don't even have to close my eyes and don't have to look behind me to know what it looked like then.

On the floor were the rows of wherries swelling out from their keelplates in a series of clinkered planks, with their riggers folded in, the back of the cox's seat loosened, the rudder laid on the duckboarding and bound round with its own rope. On the frames the long, slender racing boats with their size-coated skin, slippery as eels, resanded every year with the finest paper and revarnished dust-tight to give minimum resistance. In racks the oars, short and with a copper strip against wear for the wherries and longer with elegant tulip-shaped blades for the racing boats. The signing-out book on a small lectern, in which you had to enter for how long and with whom you were going on the river; the other books, for complaints about equipment or the behaviour of fellow-members; the mops hanging to dry on a rack, but more often to be found next to it; the corner with the dumbbells and sandbags to continue training the muscles in the winter . . . I not only remember what everything looked like in the dim light, I can even smell it.

But I know for certain that I never felt content when everything was in its place and came to rest. On the contrary. Something sad, something melancholy always took hold of me when at the end of the afternoon David and I were the last to bring our boat in, while the boat attendant had been standing impatiently on the jetty waiting for us and now quickly bolted the doors behind us. That shut out the last remaining light; it was a little dead inside now, until the next morning, when the river had woken up and the first boat was allowed out. A building goes quietly into the night. You can leave it for years with good locks on the doors and find it again just as calm and self-assured as ever. With boats it is different. They can't do without people.

Perhaps it was because I had never asked for anything unusual, anything special, had never as far as anyone knew even indicated wanting to do something impossible, that my wish to join the rowing club, many years later, met with no opposition at all from my parents. Perhaps my father was not only too astonished by my exorbitant wish, but scarcely realized what an enormous step he would have to take outside his own realm in order to fulfil it, how he would have to venture beyond the boundaries of what was fitting and safe for him.

After my first acquaintance with the river and the oarsmen I had felt myself drawn permanently and irresistibly towards the water. First mainly in my mind, because as a small child I only left the house on Sundays and, though we occasionally passed the river, and I twisted my neck and head in order not to miss a moment of its shimmering, I cannot remember its ever being the destination of one of our excursions again. Whenever we went out, the destination was always a house like ours, with windows just as small and furniture just as massive and colourless, so that if you knew no better the world inside and outside formed exact copies, reflections of each other, a closed environment from which it was impossible to escape.

When I got a little older and was sometimes allowed out

alone, I was forbidden to go further than the corners of our street. I must have stood hundreds of times in front of that imaginary line that divided Topaz Street from Emerald Street, Emerald Street with its paving stones that, as I knew only too well, flowed down broad and steady to the light, to the river. But I kept to the demarcation down to the last centimetre. I imagined that something would explode under the paving stones if I were to take a single step beyond the last gap. One of those artistic brick ornaments designed to give our street the look of an elegant whole, a utilitarian object with decorations, a brick protuberance that I came to interpret as a hostile gesture, made it impossible to look round the corner, at least if I was not to defy my parents' ban. But I imagined all the more vividly what it must look like there, I imagined I could smell the river. At that time I never gave in to my longing, I never went round the corner. I remained the pale, well-behaved child my parents wanted.

Later still I would stand for hours on the quayside looking at the waves and the ships, I would make a detour on my way to school to be able to do so, and of course I made a special study of the rowing boats and their crews. I learned to distinguish the various racing classes from each other: the eight, the coxed four and the coxless four with the man at the bow constantly looking round to set the course, especially when the boat approached the jetty of the rowing club to moor. The coxed pair with the ponderous rhythm of its oarsmen, usually big men with moustaches. The skiffs, which did not seem to have an innate character of their own but derived one completely from the man or woman operating the two oars, ploughing along laboriously, with the blades striking the water as the boat moved forwards, balancing tensely from stroke to stroke; or on the contrary hugging the water effortlessly in an elastic, natural rhythm, as if the boat itself was straining to move forwards and was pushed on a little by the waves. The double scullers, who often looked as if they were travelling faster forwards than backwards. And of course the coxless pair, the dragonfly among rowing boats, sometimes unsteady in its movements but always graceful, with oars that seemed too long for its slender hull. I got to know the teams, the boys and men who went on the water every day in all weathers because they were training for a race. The older gentlemen who met at set times, chatting away as they got in and making jokes for the first few strokes, and yet with surprising seriousness, indeed doggedness, struggling with their coordination, which was becoming ragged, with the flabby muscles, with their bellies that touched their thighs when they leaned forward, with the memory of a younger self that had been stronger and suppler. I got to know the water and its denizens so well that the desire to be one of them grew into a firm resolve, into a necessity, part of myself that could no longer be excised and so felt like a certainty, although that certainty had no foundation.

Because despite everything that became familiar, a distance remained, a dividing line that would be more difficult to cross than the one between the paving stones of Topaz Street and Emerald Street. The boundary was provisionally formed by the river itself, or more precisely, the two banks. The one I was standing on, with the fresh brick of our rented flats behind me, and the other less than two hundred metres away, with its tall trees, the houses with their extensive gardens behind and in front, only half on land and half in the water, rising up like a castle, complete with towers with banners flying, with terraces on which during the long summer evenings ladies and gentlemen gathered, straw-hatted and glasses in hand, with the gates through which the boats were carried, with its jetties and, moored to them, the pontoons which, invisible from where I was standing, bobbed on the water – there on the other bank was the clubhouse, all concrete and wood that was repainted white every spring so that it could reflect itself like a swan with new feathers – so beautiful, so elegant, so unattainable. Membership of the club was not so much barred or impossible for people on our side of the river, but was simply never something we aspired to.

Looking back, I must have felt sorry for my father, when on that weekday autumn evening he climbed the steps of that unattainable castle with me, I a step behind him with heart pounding, while he would probably have much preferred to hide behind my back. Only with hindsight can I imagine what he must have felt like during the balloting, facing four gentlemen and one lady, who treated him with the benign condescension of people who have nothing to fear from anyone, from behind the green-baize committee table covered in papers and glasses and litre bottles of beer, with shelves full of cups and other prizes behind them, bronze sculptures of water gods, silver plaques and miniatures of boats and oars. But back then I had no time for my father's feelings. I had figured it out: it was possible. I had read the rules and made enquiries. In theory anyone could join the rowing club. All I felt was the pounding of my own heart and a mixture of nerves and eagerness, because it was inconceivable, it was unthinkable for us not to pass this examination. I can't remember anything of the doubtless brief and correct answers I imagine my father gave through tight lips from behind his one and only tightly knotted tie and stand-up collar. I remember the large, complacent faces of the four men and one woman but can't remember a thing about his. I can't remember either what I replied to the question why I wanted to join the club, but I know for certain that my answer was vacuous, because in reality there were such weighty and important reasons that I could not possibly have put them into words.

Perhaps our request was so unusual and extraordinary that the committee had no arguments on which to base a refusal and hence benignly decided that I – well, why not? – should be admitted: to the club and the grounds.

II

Behind me, one of the doors of the shed swings open with a groan and immediately slams shut again. The same gust of wind blows a handful of snow or icicles into my face, and makes me squeeze my eyes shut. I try to raise my hand to my forehead and as I do so notice that the cold is already creeping into my limbs, which are starting to stiffen. It takes an effort to change position.

The doors were white like the rest of the building, but half-way up a dark-blue line had been painted along their front. Of the six doors that guarded the entrances of the boatshed in pairs, four have already completely disappeared and the other two have nothing left to hide. The shed is empty. By order of the authorities, all boathouses along the river are being demolished this winter. The reason, so they say, is that the buildings would be a hindrance in defending the city. But I can't believe that. There must be something else behind it. Even if this winter ever comes to an end, it must obviously never be summer again. No one must ever be happy again. It saddens and pleases me at the same time. It's as though one feeling has not cancelled the other out but they are reinforcing each other, joy and sorrow, just as the warm sun and the cold water can make a summer day between them, although they are completely different elements. They also say the boats have been taken to a safe place, at least the best ones, that they are strapped to beams in the attics of large mansions or are on trestles between the laundry and boxes full of old clothes and papers. I don't mind if they have to stay there for ever. The top storey of the building, which housed the club and the boardroom and the terraces where in the summer the gentlemen and their ladies drank their cider, beer and lemonade, has already been demolished. I believe the archives and the cups, the sculptures and the plates have been stored safely somewhere. Probably the accounts are still being kept and the silver may even get polished, because the club can perfectly well go on without us, even in winter, even when the building is no longer there; the club can in no time be the same as before, with new people. I don't know whether to be angry about this or resign myself to it. The club is like the river, I think for a moment, because it too goes on for ever and, like the river, will always be the same although it's always a different body of water. But I immediately reject that thought again. The river is everyone's and is always welcoming. The river has no committee. Even tonight, while the skeleton of what was once the fortress of this club creaks and the last remaining doors of the hollow shed swing and slam on their hinges, even while the river has put on a cold, angry face with rolling waves and white crests of foam and fists of wind and water, water that now and then hits the planks like a whiplash, even now I perceive the river more as an ally than as a foe. Because that cold, angry face is mine too and, like mine, it is still in motion, although it's approaching the point where movement seizes up, where molecules turn into crystals and are no longer able to reach each other, where water becomes ice and no longer flows. A river frozen is no longer a river.

It was a raw Saturday in October. I had put on my new shirt, with the blue stripe at chest height, and on top of it an ordinary woollen sweater, a pair of woollen shorts and blue plimsolls, also new. A group of boys, about ten of us, was gathered on the landing stage. The boys had put on their sports gear in the changing-room. I'd crossed the bridge in my kit. Their things were hand-me-downs, obtained from older brothers or fathers, and they wore them with the nonchalant ease that this use had created. They were just as new here as I was, but they clearly felt much more at home. David must have been among them, in that group, but I don't remember him. I don't recall any of the faces of that day. I think I looked mostly at my shoes and at the planking and I only raised my eyes when I had to.

'Head up!' shouted the man with the buttoned-up overcoat.

One by one, he made us sit down in the bank rowing tub, after which he explained the first principles of the rowing action in a businesslike tone while the others stood around in a surly circle observing the victim. The bank tub was a small wooden raft with a recess containing the rails, which were called 'slides', and a seat that could travel backwards and forwards over them. In the rigger was an oar with a blade full of holes, which meant that scarcely any pressure could be exerted on the water. You could row as hard as you liked, the raft, which was securely attached to the jetty, only moved backwards and forwards stupidly and restlessly. What counted was not putting one's back into it, but the position, the feeling.

'Head up!'

The instructor assumed that the instructions he had given to the first pupils had been absorbed by the ones following too and gradually showed less patience. But understanding a series of successive movements with your head is quite different from comprehending the same series of actions as a single movement. The body has a will and a memory of its own, located not in the brain but somewhere you can't pinpoint. It exists in the linking of muscles and sinews and bones and joints, each of which has its own past that no one knows. I was one of the last to climb onto the wobbly raft and to grab hold of the handle of the oar; two hands' distance between the thumbs, as I was told. As I went automatically backwards and forwards, out of the corner of my eye I looked at the blade full of holes. It refused to stand up straight in the water in order to be pulled through smoothly. I had to change the position of my hands. But while I was watching my hands, I realized that my back was not flexing in the prescribed way and as I realized this it was already too late and I was forgetting the acute angle in lifting the blade out of the water and realized that I had allowed myself too little space between my abdomen and thighs, because I had remained hanging forward over my oar.

A chilly autumn wind was blowing, but I immediately started sweating. It must have been noticeable, straight through my new shirt with the blue stripe, a shirt taken out of its tissue paper only an hour before. That evening I was to practise the movement sitting on my bed, naked, with my arms and legs stretched, and casting strange shadows on the walls of my narrow room, but here under the wide October sky on that raft which was moving but not moving forwards, I was immediately and painfully aware that if there was such a thing as a natural talent in the rowing field, I did not have it. Doggedly and red-faced from the effort, I tried to copy what I had seen in the way in which it had been explained.

'Head up!'

As long as I rowed, there was something odd about my posture. At the end of the stroke I bent my upper body over the oar as though I didn't really want to let go of the water, with my shoulders tense and my head bent over my labour. I wanted to do my best and didn't realize that the best people simply stand above everything and experience work not as work but as an affirmation of their potential.

The chaos in my body was nothing compared with the chaos that eight bodies can cause collectively. It was a week later, our first acquaintance with open water. The same grey sky, the same raw wind, now and again a touch of rain. The oar that each of us had in his hands had become a wild animal; it had become an enemy that, straight and rigid as it was, seemed to curl to escape its possessor, while beneath us the boat behaved very much in the same way, like a sea snake shaking its back at unexpected moments and lurching to left or right with a snap, while the opposite side reared up with the same speed and threatened to skin a few fingers. I tried to tell myself that rowing was something mechanical and that the boat was not a living being but an instrument that one should be able to play in a rational fashion, but I couldn't find my way among the instructions which I had learned by heart and was now repeating to myself in an attempt to regain my composure, the composure of my body. I don't know if the others were thinking the same, but they seemed to be. I could feel it. For the first time, though without being aware of it, I experienced how other people's bodies communicated themselves to the boat with all their faults and clumsy movements, and with all the power which they tried at the wrong moment to transmit to the water through their arms and legs, through their backs and oars. Perhaps without us the boat was not a living being, but as soon as we had taken possession of it the thing definitely acquired a will of its own. The quirky behaviour we had to endure was the result of our helplessness. The unpredictability of wood and metal was nothing but a lack of control over our own bodies and a lack of co-ordination of our bodies with each other. Now and again, a high wave rolled in over the side of the boat. My feet became soaked in the new plimsolls, my sweater absorbed the water and a splash over my hands made it even harder to keep the wood from escaping between my fingers. I felt my self-doubt beginning to churn and I tried to suppress the feeling forcibly, leaning even more deeply over my oar.

The man in the buttoned-up coat had squeezed his way into the cox's seat; the tails of his coat hung on either side of the boat and quickly darkened. By counting loudly he indicated when we were expected, in perfect time, to put the blade in the water and at the same time exert pressure.

After a while he began correcting each of us separately, shouting instructions accompanied by a number corresponding to our place in the boat. I sat in the last position but one, where the boat narrowed back towards the bow, and yet my number was called out more often than any of the others and the more often it was called, to attract attention repeatedly to the same errors, the more I felt my despair mounting. I wished I could merge into the group. If any mistakes were made they would be joint mistakes, not my personal responsibility. Each time my number was called out, I flinched. The vision of the eight rowers emerging in complete harmony from under the bridge seemed more unattainable than ever. Did everyone here realize by now that I was the only hindrance on the path to perfect teamwork, the pale and clumsy obstacle barring the way to harmony, to the natural order of things? Hadn't they long since decided to continue together, without me? I remember that feeling as if it were yesterday, because it returned periodically at all later stages of my life on the water, particularly when things went badly, without the cause of our problems ever being entirely clear. I always remained terrified of not belonging where I most loved to be.

Of course that fear was unnecessary and exaggerated. The others probably felt much the same as I did during that first outing. Their nonchalance, their grown-up wisecracks had disappeared the moment the boat was pushed off from the raft and we tried to row the first stroke. If I had dared to take my eyes off the seat of the boy in front of me as it travelled incessantly back and forth over the gleaming metal rails, I would have seen six pairs of backs and shoulders and arms ahead of me, toiling to and fro like so many humps on our water creature, showing every degree of curvature and stiffening, with the blades of the oars disappearing into the waves not simultaneously but one after the other, sometimes almost colliding. And yet, although none of us could pay it any attention at that moment, preoccupied as we were with all the difficulties we had to surmount, together we created a minor miracle. In spite of everything, the prow of the boat ploughed through the waves, sometimes even trembling for an instant as if dreaming of a smoother passage, of real speed. In spite of everything, the boat was in motion.

In the course of that first autumn and that first winter I gradually got to know the boys with whom I took to the water every Saturday. High-school pupils, fellows who would go into the family business and so had no time for any further education, sickly-looking types with curved backs who needed to improve their condition, or future men of independent means already suffering from obesity. Almost all of them had loud voices. David was the quiet one with dark curls who invariably sat behind the stroke and, pulling calmly on his oar, had to support the pace set. I stood out too – by never saying anything at all. Occasionally I felt there was some improvement in the way we propelled the boat forwards, but on other afternoons it was clear that we were rowing even worse than the week before. It also became increasingly obvious that there was no solution in sight to such a huge tangle of interrelated factors. Eight boys were struggling with their arms and legs and when they were not doing that, they were struggling with each other. Or so it seemed, because of course all these difficulties occurred at once, those within ourselves and those within the unit as a whole. But just as there are drawings in which you can see a depiction of one thing or another, but never of both at the same time, it was still impossible to feel coherently and concentrate on a solution to everything at once. Meanwhile the man in the buttoned-up coat simply continued issuing instructions to us collectively and individually, but I began to suspect that this approach did not spring from an understanding of the whole and an analysis into parts, but rather was a matter of habit. He was just improvising.

Probably it was also habit that made him give the order to increase power and strike rate more and more often. This usually led to even greater chaos, which now also manifested itself as pain. Pain in your shoulders, your back and your hands. Blisters that burst, so that you felt a slippery colourless liquid, thinner than blood and thicker than water, creep between your fingers and the wood of the oar.

But even then I recall an occasional sensation, with which I would later become more familiar. It was as if in picking up speed the boat sometimes accelerated by itself and wanted to carry us along with it and became tolerant of our mistakes, which grew less glaring, less significant, the faster the movements were executed. This caused us a brief, strange surge of joy.

My lack of confidence did not decrease as the weeks progressed and grew into months. Rather, I got used to it, just as I did to the soaking-wet kit over which I buttoned my jacket to run home across the bridge when training was over. The others, I knew, had washed communally under the row of hot showers in the men's changing-room, the steam from which pumped out into the cold winter's air through the ventilation bricks, and then had a cup of tea in the club for a few cents. It was not only out of shyness that I kept apart. Mainly I felt that this exuberant sociability was hard to reconcile with our hopeless exhibitions on the water, with all the incorrect movements of which I was painfully aware even as I was making them, and with my own inadequacy, to which was now added the sensation of insufficient muscular strength. I had the constant suspicion that I might be the hitherto undiscovered defective cog-wheel in our machine, and that once I was removed things were bound to go smoothly. I felt I hadn't deserved any reward.

The new year began, there was ice on the water and our instructor pointed to a cardboard sheet that hung in the shed on which were simple line drawings of a figure doing a series of exercises for strengthening various groups of muscles. I learned the exercises by heart and did them every evening before I went to bed and every morning before I got dressed; feet on the ice-cold linoleum, at first shivering in my vest but getting warmer and warmer as the programme progressed. With my ankles hooked under the edge of the bed I raised myself from a lying position until my nose touched my knees and I repeated this a hundred times. After I had folded up the bed there was room to do press-ups, first twenty, later thirty and forty repetitions. I exerted static strength against the doorpost, turning red in the face as I did so. Static strength suited our house best. The walls of my room were too thin for jumping and too narrow for making windmill movements with my arms.

In the afternoons I spent a long time standing on the quayside and saw hundreds of people gliding across the expanse of ice. The river had become a completely different space, more a palatial room than a landscape. And it sounded like one too: the scratching of the skates in the dry air could just as well have been high heels on marble; there was music; people gave little yelps of pleasure. There was even eating and drinking. Occasionally I saw a couple of familiar faces among the skaters, boys from the boat, but I had neither the inclination nor the courage to raise my hand.

Spring came. We resumed our training. There were one or two new faces in the crew and there was something that resembled a race, two sets of eight boys and their screaming coxes careering side by side down a stretch of the river under a lowering sky, pounding the water and coughing. It didn't surprise me that we lost. By this time the instructor had given up his cox's seat to someone of our own age, a small, rotund boy who took great pleasure in tying a brass megaphone in front of his mouth and counting off each of our strokes separately. The coach now cycled with us along the bank. Without an overcoat, dressed only in a sports jacket. And then, one day, just in shirt-sleeves with rolled-up cuffs.

I remember that day because without any explanation or announcement we suddenly saw someone else cycling by his side, someone who made a striking contrast with the familiar figure of our customary instructor. The stranger was a heavily built man, as could be seen clearly even from a distance, and where our coach was perhaps rather frivolous in hanging his sports jacket over the handlebars of his bicycle, the stranger had gone to the opposite extreme by keeping on a black winter coat with what on closer inspection looked suspiciously like a fur collar. His bike was also out of the ordinary for that matter and made an unusually sporty impression with this cyclist on it; it was light grey with white tyres and had large brake levers on the handlebars. A foreign model. When we tied up he was standing waiting for us, with two calf-skin shoes precisely on the edge of the landing stage. He looked even bigger close up. The collar really was fur. We waited before getting out of the boat and observed him curiously.

'Boys,' said our instructor, who had stayed in the background. 'Boys . . .' and he said nothing else, but made a gesture like a master of ceremonies introducing a music-hall act.

There was a moment's silence. The enormous man had opened his coat and under it appeared a shiny waistcoat into whose pockets he tucked both thumbs before introducing himself.

'Schneiderhahn. Alfred Schneiderhahn. Doktor Alfred Schneiderhahn.'

As he uttered these last words he made a slight bow – actually more a nod of satisfaction. Then he walked along the boat until he got to where David was sitting, took a thumb out of his waistcoat pocket and pointed with a vague gesture in his direction. Then he nodded again, as if to say 'Yes, I mean you', turned round and, casually stepping over the protruding oars, walked back until he was facing me. I raised my head and he gave me that same nod, indicating 'And you'. There was a moment's astonished silence among the others. But as soon as the fur coat, with Doktor Schneiderhahn in it, began heading in the direction of the club, the first stifled quip was heard, from the mouth of a scrawny, ginger-haired jeweller's son. As the usual silly bout of laughter and giggling broke out around me, I was seized by an almost hallowed feeling, as though it wasn't a fat stranger, probably a German, but a high priest who was walking off to drink a *café au lait* and a glass of cognac in the club after selecting me for a mission whose purpose I did not even know. My premonition was correct, although I didn't yet know just how accurate it was to prove. With that nod of the head, with that slight tug on the rudder, Schneiderhahn changed the direction of my life.

My parents never asked about my experiences on the water and I never told them anything. It was as though by saying nothing about my Saturday visits to the club they were trying to neutralize their effects. I don't know if they noticed the exercises that I did twice a day. They could scarcely help doing so. But they said nothing. I had the impression that they regarded the fulfilment of the ambition that had taken root in me so many years earlier as a sickness that must be allowed to run its course, a cancerous growth that would wither of its own accord for lack of nourishment. Of course, exactly the opposite was true. I had discovered that my intuition of thirteen, fourteen years, an eternity ago, was true: there was space and life out there; the roof that the housing corporation had given us not only offered protection, it also shut out light and air.

I never even heard my father say anything about his visit to the committee room. I don't think he regarded it as a humiliation. I don't even think he gave it much thought later. For him, it must have been the confirmation of what he already thought he knew: we would never thrive in those surroundings – more a reassurance than a reason for disquiet.

At the end of that first rowing year, they were given a hint that they were mistaken, that my affliction wouldn't blow over but would get worse and worse. It was the first time I didn't accompany them to the bathhouse.

The bathhouse was an octagonal building erected in our district at the intersection of Emerald and Diamond Streets. Our visits were among the few fixed rituals in our otherwise sober existence. Every Saturday, towards the end of the afternoon, my mother took three towels, a comb and two halves of the same flaky bar of soap and put them in a wicker bag. My father and I, coats and scarves on, were already waiting in the hall and opened the door as soon as she joined us. The space by the front door was too small for three people, so somebody had to exit whenever a third person arrived, which made hesitation on the threshold impossible and superfluous. Having been expelled by the built-in intestinal contractions of our house, our family began moving in the direction of the building with the fresh red-tiled roof at the end of the street. I expect my mother sometimes said something cheerful about the convenience of the proximity of a modern hygienic facility. My father said nothing, until we paid our five cents and turned right down the corridor to the men's section.

Then he handed me our piece of soap and pointed to the door of the shower cubicle and pronounced the words 'Fresh just for you'. Always the same joke. Maybe he sometimes left it out, but he must have said it so often that in my memory it is inextricably bound up with the ritual. I don't even know exactly what it meant – fresh soap? A freshly cleaned cubicle? Jets of fresh water? – but I never experienced our visits to the bathhouse as having anything to do with freshness or coolness. I would encounter the soap the same evening back in our kitchen again, next to the dirty dishes, and it was quite evident that the bathing cubicle was used by scores of other people every day. After every shower it was wiped clean and brushed out, but anyone who looked carefully could see in the niches and across the tiles from chest height upwards a greyish film of soap deposits mixed with dirt and grease. I tried not to look, although every time my eyes were drawn irresistibly towards the gunge. I also preferred not to look at my body, which, completely naked and in the cold light of the high, narrow windows, looked even greyer than at home, half-dressed. After I had soaked myself I looked at my feet as my ration of warm water descended on me, and followed the water sliding away through my toes towards the drainhole. A little later my father's feet would stand in the same

36

spot, feet like mine, with collapsed insteps and red marks from shoes tied too tightly. And if nothing changed and I had a son, his feet would also stand here one day.

Feet. I never wanted to think about the rest of my father's body. From my feet upwards, I wanted to be different from him.

On Saturday evenings we ate an hour later than on other days. Since nothing else needed to happen and indeed nothing else ever did happen to us, Saturday evenings were a high point in my parents' life. They had got through another week, and had finally reached the day of rest in safety. The visit to the bathhouse was the last item in the schedule of duties. As our hair dried, an intermission in our life began. 'Finally, some peace and quiet,' said my mother. My father sighed and put the radio on. He liked dance music, the kind announced by a velvety voice, in which even the trumpets manage to sound velvety against the background of a discreet rhythm section and smooching violins. Even the magic eye in the radio seemed half-closed this evening. My parents liked dance music, but not dancing. On Saturday evenings their life was in equilibrium.

The fact that I no longer wanted to go with them to the bathhouse one day must have come as a shock to them, comparable to the refusal of other children to continue going to church on Sundays. A direct attack on the values of safety, security and rest.

But I'd already had a shower in the afternoon, at the club, I said one Saturday at the beginning of summer, hastily and in a feigned businesslike tone. I turned quickly and went into my bedroom, as if I had something to do there. I just had time to see my father's face contorted in pain, my mother's wide-eyed astonishment. For a moment I thought he'd follow me and try to dissuade me, but he didn't, and I should have known he wouldn't. My father was a man who hung his head when he was beaten. This time the blow was twice as hard, because it came from me.

Leaning back against the door of the room, I listened intently to the sounds from the hall. Stifled muttering, coats being put on, the sliding of the front-door bolt. Then for a while nothing, before the door opened and shut again. I was no longer one of them. The hall was now big enough for the whole family.

David shook hands with me before we took to the water together for the first time and as he did so surveyed me with a look that I was to come to know so well: a mixture of irony and sincerity, one tempered by the other, creating a sense of both distance and warmth, which besides a gesture towards the other person was a confirmation of his own unap-proachability. He did it because we were temporary part-ners and I took it as an expression of his willingness to make the best of it. That was sporting of him. Alongside the land-ing stage lay the incredibly slender shape of a coxless pair. Doktor Schneiderhahn had had it brought down for us from one of the top racks. The brass gates shone with a matt glow in the sun, the oars lay crossways over the slides and seats. Schneiderhahn had first had the boat laid on sling trestles and had given it a checkover. With a large white handker-chief – literally everything about the man was enormous – he brushed some dust off the milky-white skin. Then he

took a leather case out of his coat pocket and from that a pro-
tractor and a spirit level, with which he twice measured the
angle of the riggers, the number of degrees by which it
diverged from the right angle, once along the riggers themselves and the second time along the edge of the blade,
which was forced down firmly into the gate by David and
myself as though we were making a stroke. 'It will have to
do,' was the Doktor's opinion and he motioned to us that
we could put the boat into the water.

I still don't know how we reached the bend where the
path along the river began and Schneiderhahn was waiting
for us on his racing bike. As we moved forwards, the blades
of our oars dragged across the water looking for support
and, when the moment came for them to turn to the vertical
and catch the water, a feeling comparable to vertigo flooded
my body. The water of the river was as opaque as it had
always been, but now it suddenly also seemed bottomless.
Only the stroke itself offered a little support, but it lasted for
a mere instant and then that instability at the end was back
again, when the blade had to relinquish its support. And that
was just the feeling transmitted by my hands.

Meanwhile an overpowering dome of air, sky and water
at which I dared not even look opened up before me,
becoming wider and wider the further the safe haven of the
landing stage and jetty lay behind us. I had always seen the
back and shoulders of someone else in front of me when we
were rowing and it would have seemed natural if I had
now had David's figure ahead of me. But David rowed
starboard, and stroke position on this boat was for a port-
side oarsman. I could feel his eyes in my back and his usu-

ally friendly expression must have soon given way to irritation at my fumbling. It wasn't so bad now that I had to choose the tempo and rhythm for myself. In fact it meant one problem less, that of synchronizing. But the dizzying emptiness in front of me, towards which I had to move at each stroke, was something I couldn't get used to immediately. It was as if in those first hundred metres that we rowed together I was released into a new universe.

It was David's job to look round every so often and keep us on course. The length of board on which his right foot rested was equipped for this purpose with a revolving section attached via cables to the rudder. Obviously even he found this new task a problem. 'Hold it there,' he said suddenly, but neither of us dared to stop abruptly by turning the blade upright in the water and hence we struck a mooring post quite hard with his rigger. 'Uh oh,' said David drily. And then after a short inspection of the rigger frame, on which nothing was obviously twisted, he brought the boat back on course with a couple of short strokes and indicated that I should continue. 'Off we go again.' His voice always sounded calm. I felt myself trembling to my very depths as we went under the bridge. And on the bend, I knew, the great Schneiderhahn was waiting, bicycle in hand.

I was already convinced that Doktor Schneiderhahn had been wrong when he had selected me as well as David to go on rowing under his supervision in the queen of competitions. But of course he couldn't give any inkling of that halfway through our first outing; a certain politeness obliged David and him to complete this practice run. Not only was he a master, but when it came down to it he might also be a kind person, this Doktor Schneiderhahn. His mastery was shown in the brief but lucid instructions that he gave as he observed us, doubtless shaking his head. His accent was heavy, but the tone he used was so calm and at the same time so forceful that it was impossible not to follow his instructions. After the first kilometre we somehow produced a couple of strokes that really propelled the boat along and even succeeded for a moment in no longer putting the brakes on ourselves by letting the blades trail in the water between strokes.

Schneiderhahn didn't pay compliments. When he said nothing, he was satisfied, and when he had been silent for a while he tried something new. After the turning-point, he made us do exercises to improve the balance. Half-way through travelling forwards, we had to stop and see how long we could keep our blades free of the water. Not long. A little later he ordered us to put more power into it. For a couple of strokes it went well. Out of the corner of my eye I saw the reeds going past faster, and with my legs, my shoulders and my back I pushed the water harder and harder away from me. Then it was as if what I had been holding on to was suddenly wrenched from my hands, the blade dived down and tried to pull the oar parallel with the boat, the side tipped and we shipped water. David threw his body in the other direction and I instinctively did the same while grabbing wildly at the handle of my oar. The boat shifted back and forth and then gradually righted itself. We had come to a stop at an oblique angle to the direction we were travelling in.

'That', said David, 'was a crab.' I'd never heard the

expression before but I immediately understood what he meant. So the way my oar had suddenly changed from a reliable tool into a treacherous creature with a will of its own that plunged into the depths at lightning speed was called a crab. It was typical that David should immediately know the right name for what happened to us. But something in his voice nevertheless betrayed the fact that he was alarmed too. 'And we nearly got a ducking,' he said, his composure almost complete. Nevertheless, I took it as a reproach.

Schneiderhahn ignored the incident. 'Go on rowing,' he said. 'Row on!' Hesitantly I moved forwards again and with arms trembling I made my blade re-engage with the water, feeling that every stroke from now on was first and foremost a new opportunity for capsizing. The blade at first moved awkwardly back and forth like a fish that had been on dry land or in a net and was now regaining its freedom, and then I felt it again assuming its vertical position and myself regaining a grip and the beginnings of confidence.

'And head *hoch*!' cried Schneiderhahn.

A few weeks later we got a ducking after all. After our first training session was over, Doktor Schneiderhahn had said nothing except 'See you tomorrow' and David had looked at me with his dark eyes in his usual way and shrugged his shoulders. From then on we rowed five times a week, every day except Wednesdays and Sundays. After a few times we really got better; sometimes we rowed ten strokes or more without our blades touching the waves in between; we got used to the exhausted feeling in our muscles after training was over, a sign that we'd really done something and that we'd done it right, and we discovered that feeling hadn't entirely disappeared when we set off again the following day. I also gradually got used to the idea that the great coach might not have been wrong, that he really saw something in the improbable combination of David and me, or else that he was too stubborn to admit his mistake for the time being.

Schneiderhahn had begun by getting us to unlearn an old-fashioned form of rowing, in which the back was held stiff and moved backwards and forwards like a wedge so that the shock of each impact went through the whole of the upper body like a blow. 'We shall be rowing one hundred per cent Fairbairn,' the coach announced. That meant crouching like a tiger, the back bent flexibly long before the water was caught with a rapid movement, then during the stroke uncoiling the back so that the pressure moved gradually from the legs to the chest, the arms and the shoulders. Only the last section, the space to allow the hands to turn and push away, became more difficult rather than easier in this way.

It must have been at the end of the second or the third week that we went into the water. Not during a series of hard strokes, but after the training session was over, while we were rowing home tired and almost satisfied; not in the middle of the river, but a few metres from the landing stage and the club, where it was busy that afternoon. It was probably a Saturday and in any case the weather was glorious. David looked over his shoulder and warned me to row more calmly, he himself made a last firm stroke so as to approach the landing stage at the right angle. At that moment the gate locking the rigger at the top came loose. His oar shot up and the boat began slowly but inexorably, almost elegantly, to list to stroke side. Automatically I pulled my feet out of the leather flaps fastened with strong laces on the stretcher as I felt the water sliding up along my body, first with a splash and then gradually sucking into my clothes. My head scarcely went under. I looked to where David's head popped up next to me, suddenly without curls. Even now, he managed to assume not only a surprised but also a rather ironic expression. Then I looked at the bank, where a peal of mocking laughter had rung out. The boys with whom until a few weeks ago we had been rowing in an eight had gathered on the landing stage and couldn't contain their glee at the ducking the star duo had got. A few older members stood on the bank, grinning, and among them I saw Doktor Schneiderhahn, who had put his bike on the stand and now hurried up to us. When he saw what had happened, he stopped, he opened his sports jacket and with his thumbs hooked into his waistcoat he laughed loudest of all, a warm thundering laugh, the first time we'd seen him so cheerful. As we swam, we pushed the boat and the oar that had come loose to the side and there David hauled himself up, his shirt and his shorts dragging behind him like loose-fitting skin. He was laughing too, silently but with a broad grin, despite the cut on his forehead from which a slow, watery trickle of blood was now issuing. I looked at him and I joined in after a fashion.

But even before we were able to take off our wet clothes, Schneiderhahn called us over, serious again now, and waved a fat finger in front of our faces. 'What do we learn from this? That the practice session is not over until the boat is safely back inside on the rack! Not after the last hard stroke, not even when you're alongside. Only when the boat is dried off and put away! *Disziplin, meine Herren*, nothing will be achieved without discipline!' We nodded, of course we nodded, still dripping wet.

I learned something else that afternoon: not to be frightened of the water. Or rather: I learned that it wasn't the water I had been afraid of. The water was wet and slightly cold, precisely as you might expect. What I had really been afraid of was upsetting the balance, the unstable construction of trust that existed between myself and David, the wood and metal of the boat, the water of the river and the eye of the Doktor on the shore. It was a trust that I still couldn't really believe in, but the collapse of which I already felt would be a real disappointment, a bath colder than the river could ever give. The laughter of David and the laughter of Schneiderhahn had assured me that no real accident had occurred and that even the spiteful guffawing of the bystanders, about which I would otherwise probably have been deeply unhappy and from which I would have slunk away, hadn't got through to me. On the contrary, I'd even laughed back a little. I had been strong. The water had turned out to be my friend. Looking back on it, I felt as if that afternoon, having grown up as an unbeliever, I had been baptized.

Schneiderhahn was always clear in his instructions. They were simple, easy to understand. So why did it take me so long to understand a movement not just with my brain, but also with the muscles that had to execute it? I knew exactly what I had to do the moment the stroke was completed and the blade left the water – quick movement of the wrist towards my lap, bringing my shoulders back at the same time and relaxing them, letting my back collapse to make room for my hands, pushing the hands quickly away from me and then at the point when the arms were extended, beginning to move forwards slowly and in a controlled way. A simple series of actions that had to be carried out as a single movement. It was weeks, months before I occasionally performed the movement correctly. And when I managed it, it was precisely at the moment when I wasn't thinking about it and was no longer repeating the cycle in my head. It was as if that piece of consciousness had then finally left the cells of my brain and arrived where it belonged, in a fibre or a muscle. But sometimes it disappeared again and the body had obviously suddenly forgotten what it had known. Then nothing went right. While my head tried to repeat its instructions, the body acted dumb. 'Shoulders loose! Head *hoch*!' shouted Schneiderhahn from the bank for the umpteenth time. The blade of my oar got caught in the waves and couldn't possibly be got out of the water again. Hands, shoulders, arms, knees – each went their own way independently of the other. A difference between the consciousness of the body and that of the head is that the former can experience panic, but fortunately cannot know despair.

So I was sure that my limbs had a form of consciousness. I could even sometimes feel where it was situated. But how do two bodies learn a single movement together? Where is the knowledge that they have gathered between the two of them? Every movement that we made in the slender boat, we made together. A series of actions was not singular but always double and interwoven, every gesture of my hand or my wrist influenced the hands and the wrists of David, and a single movement of his broad shoulders could compensate a little for the nervous jerk that I gave mine at the end of a stroke. If we had not only a separate consciousness in our bodies, but also had together built up a quantity of knowledge which consisted in part of David and in part of Anton, however improbable that combination seemed at first sight, then where was that joint element located?

For a while I thought that it must in be the boat itself, which we, the moment we put our oars in the riggers, sat down on the seats and put the straps on our feet, injected as it were with our jointly amassed knowledge, just as a battery is charged by poles, positive and negative, which can only provide energy together. But I eventually abandoned that thought. Wood, brass and metal conducted our strength, that was true, otherwise we couldn't have fought the water. But it struck me as improbable that the boat also added something and was the carrier of our joint ability. It had to be something that happened directly between us. Sometimes it was as if I could feel David's arms and legs, as if the boat between us disappeared. If it was to have any chance of success, our movement must issue from a joint memory, but that memory was created only at the beginning of the movement and when the movement ceased, our experience was nothing more than the vague notion of something that seemed sweet and effortless and so extra-ordinary that it couldn't be repeated in words and perhaps not even in actions.

Yet we continued to strive stubbornly for this. Before we succeeded even once in producing a series of strokes and in covering a reasonable distance in a naturally flowing rhythm, we knew that something of the kind must be possible. Otherwise we would not have taken the daily trouble, not been able to cope with the floundering around, not defied despair; otherwise I would have long ago stopped trying to provide my reluctant body with a perfect memory.

Was it coincidence that there were no witnesses when we finally succeeded for the first time? Schneiderhahn was sometimes suddenly absent for a few days. He would inform us briefly after the training session that he 'had to attend to business' in another town and hand us a sheet of squared paper with instructions and schedules for the next few days. 'Anton-David' was written at the top of the sheet with an elegant hyphen. Below it were a series of figures and a few words, the name of the exercise and the number of repetitions, and finally, always preceded by an artistic paragraph sign, a number of instructions of a more general nature. 'Anton: keep your head up and collapse far backwards' – that was seldom missing.

Schneiderhahn's handwriting was characterized by high loops and letters which continued downwards in a strange way as though there were a little step on them. '*Sütterlin*,' said David, folding the paper into strips and putting it between the bolts of his steering gear in the sole of his right shoe. 'We've got tons of books in that script at home.' I found it difficult to read and was glad that David had taken the task on. He always announced the next exercise in his calm, deep voice, and I was allowed to say 'Yes' just before the beginning of the first stroke.

It was a sunny day in May, unusually warm for the time of year, but there was something restless in the air when we pushed off from the landing stage, got into position, and, in order to find the coordination and balance, made a couple of quarter and half strokes and then tried to take the boat on to our legs in a calm tempo. High in the sky the clouds were scudding quicker than the small breath of wind down here below could justify. The waves were small but the water was restless and after the new bridge, ours, the one with its electric lamps that also marked the edge of the city, there was suddenly a treacherous cross-current, as though a freighter with a powerful engine had passed, or a tug. But there was no motorboat to be seen, we passed only a flat-bottomed barge with a large brown sail, from the look of it loaded with crates of vegetables, and a pair of yawls. Despite the waves, which now came first from the right and then from the left and nudged us stubbornly off balance, I tried to make a firm stroke so that we would be nice and warm when we did the first exercises. And so we rounded the first bend, more a kink in the river called the Omval, at a reasonable speed. As we came to that point I always felt the emptiness of the countryside that we were now approaching in my back. The waves became different and I smelled the sickly-sweet scent of cocoa from the factory on a side canal. It must be terrible for the people who live nearby to smell chocolate day and night, but we passed the smell like a beacon, a familiar outpost of the harbour. Even now, when I smell cocoa it makes me think of the river, and when I think of the river, I smell cocoa again. Sometimes I imagined the smell flowing into Emerald Street late in the evening, turning the corner and reaching my bedroom window. Or perhaps it really did happen occasionally. Light can only travel in a straight line, but smell and water can make turns. After the Omval, the river is at its widest for a while.

We passed the last sheds and isolated villas still belonging to the city and went through our first exercises. Schneiderhahn had views that were not shared by anyone, and methods not used by anyone else. Perhaps that was why he had been given two beginners to coach and wasn't allowed to get involved with the experienced teams in the club. But it was also possible that he wanted to prove his point by working precisely with us, so that it couldn't be said to him later that the foundation for success had already been laid by someone else. To tell the truth, we never concerned ourselves with the question of whether Schneiderhahn was right. For us, his authority was never in any doubt. And so we almost never travelled the usual long stretches at an average tempo, intended to 'engrave' the stroke pattern, which often gives the rowing of young teams a look of desperate drudgery, but we faithfully carried out the '*fartlek*', in which we rowed alternately hard and gently, in an ascending series, ten hard, ten light, twenty hard, twenty light – up to fifty, after which you counted back down again.

'*Fahrtspiel*!' Schneiderhahn was wont to announce from

his bike in a festive tone, as if he had a special treat in store for us. In reality it was a gruelling business: an explosion of power during the hard strokes and no opportunity to ease off during the gentle ones, because it was crucial to keep the balance and the rhythm exactly, or if necessary restore them. In this way strength and concentration were trained in quick succession. And competitiveness too, because the end of each series that you counted off in your mind meant a minor finish that you wanted to reach without weakening. It tired us out completely, but after we had reached an imaginary finish line for the last time, there was always a great feeling of satisfaction. We had not only covered a distance, we had accomplished a task *en route*.

During these training sessions, the landscape by the side of the water was part of the work. The reeds, the meadows, the farms and, further away from the city, the gazebos behind which country houses, white and grey, had stood dreaming for hundreds of years – they actually had nothing to do with the two sweating boys moving over the water, sometimes groaning and cursing (myself), sometimes looking round and adjusting the steering, holding back or putting extra effort into it (David). But they were nevertheless indispensable. It seemed as if all that nature and those traces of civilization were there specially for us, as a backdrop to elements of our work, just as we, conversely, worked up a sweat in gratitude for the privilege of being able to be part of it. The two of us in a narrow brown boat, on the glassy water, which appeared first black and then blue again, lit by a burning sun, nodded to by overhanging trees, encouraged by whispering grass and whistling reeds, stared at by cows and fishermen, with the bleating of sheep or the foghorn of a freighter in our ears, with the wind stroking through our hair and our lungs filled with oxygen. Whoever did his best could sooner or later expect his reward from this landscape.

We usually turned before the bridge of the first village after the city, two kilometres or so past the municipal boundary post, and shortly after that turning-point something began to change around us. It was still warm. But there was also moisture in the air. Smells that were more powerful and spicy. A slight breeze, a momentary ripple across the waves. Immediately afterwards the water became motionless. Without saying anything, I let the stroke become more powerful and raised the strike rate. I wanted to get home before the rain, but the river itself, with its inviting, smooth surface, also demanded more strength. David understood and followed. Even as we were gradually accelerating over that improbably smooth surface I saw a dense band of rain bearing down on us, a mysterious curtain swaying hypnotically as it approached us, like the cloak of a huge, invisible wizard. And along with it a sweet, heavy odour, different from the one just now, which must be the smell of the rain itself. Plants and trees bowed their heads, in the enamel of the water there suddenly appeared billions of little pockmarks, but before I could take it all in, it was upon us and the rain descended, a haze in which the fine drops could not be distinguished individually but gave us a sense of being completely enveloped. I put my back into it. David followed. Nothing remained dry. I felt my shirt wrinkling heavily around me, I felt the water in my drenched shoes. I saw my arms swing forwards as if by themselves and place the oar in the water with an impatience that I had never known before. My shoulders eagerly took up the weight and my legs immediately pushed off. Effortlessly the blade left the water at the end of the stroke and described a perfect little arc between chest and knees. My head leaned back in pleasure for a fraction of a second before I took a deep breath and moved forwards again behind my arms. I looked straight ahead and no longer saw the alarmingly ethereal emptiness of air, sky and water which had once made me feel giddy, but something that gave me support and confidence. And inexhaustible energy. I stepped up the intensity a little further, without thinking but in the right way, not by raising the tempo but by exerting more force so that the movement itself demanded a higher tempo. David followed. It was unnaturally quiet around us. The only thing we heard was the all-penetrating rush of the rain and through it, in the foreground, the violent crack with which we hit the water and the deeper, rather hollow sound with which our blades left it perfectly in time. Or was it not the rain that was rushing around us, but my own blood, our own breathing? I couldn't hear David panting behind me. That must mean that our breath had the same cadence, that his heartbeat was in sync with mine. I imagined how the pointed, brass-covered bow of our boat was shooting through the water, dipping for an instant as we engaged our blades and then moving forwards in an upward diagonal, diving, accelerating. Past the grass, past the reeds, like a young pike that is pursuing a prey just under the surface of the water which can no longer escape it, watched from the dark depths by the common mass of slowly snapping fish. But of course I wasn't thinking in similes, because everything happened automatically. I felt the water streaming through my hair and over my face. If I had wanted to cry, I wouldn't have noticed.

In a moment the rain had gone and immediately the sun was shining again, as if it had never been away, and perhaps that was the case, because even during the shower it remained remarkably light and warm. As the last drops fell, more from the branches and the leaves along the bank than from the sky, I reduced our speed with long strokes. It had lasted five, perhaps six minutes in all. The surface was now broken only by the lonely trail of puddles we'd left in it, which remained visible for a long time in the still water before I saw it fade on a gentle bend and become one with the river again. My skin was tingling. Here and there a bird began singing hesitantly. Behind me, I heard David.

'Mmm,' he said, revelling in the experience.

The summer months were warm and went on for ever. David had packed his bags, his tennis racquets, the English novels which made his sister laugh so much (but which he also sometimes read, he admitted magnanimously) and had departed for Switzerland with his family. Schneiderhahn had also left town and this time his business required more than a few days. We wouldn't see him until September, he said, he was travelling south, but he was relying on us to keep our muscles in shape during the summer and gave us the date and time when he expected us back on the landing stage. Healthy, in sports gear and *pünktlich* – implying that suddenly, after more than two months, there wasn't another minute to lose. He said all this as if it were completely obvious that even after the summer, in the new season, we would organize our free time completely around his requirements, and of course he was absolutely right. David agreed with a shrug of his shoulders, but his shrug was as reliable as somebody else's fervent oath. I probably nodded enthusiastically and said yes a little too eagerly, but that was because I was rejoicing inwardly.

I had turned seventeen at the beginning of that summer, which meant that I now had a job in an office. It's a part of my life that I can't say anything about. Not because it filled me with revulsion, but simply because there's nothing to say about it. The office was on a canal, invoices were written and dockets counted, the post was brought round and pencils were sharpened. It was cool and, in the cellar next to the warehouse, damp as well. The hours I spent there were necessary but not significant, just like the combing of my hair or the cleaning of my teeth in the morning at the washbasin under the shaving mirror which had belonged to my grandfather.

The best part of the day was early in the morning when I left home. I set off in good time, so that I would be able to make a detour. I hurried round the corner. In Emerald Street I could already smell the river. I crossed the road and forced myself not to look too intently at the water, although of course I cast sideways glances and it was immediately obvious to me what state it was in, calm or troubled, quiet or busy. I didn't turn left towards the centre of town but right, until I got to the new bridge with the electric lamps.

In the middle of the bridge I stopped and only then did I allow myself, with my arms resting on the wrought iron of the balustrade, to look properly into the water, first directly beneath me, black in the shadow of the pillars, and then slowly further away, where it became blue and white and began to shimmer, as far as I could see.

I took in everything: the freight barges on their way into the centre of town or on the contrary returning after delivering their cargo to the markets, the life on the houseboats, the flags on the larger ships, the washing hanging out to dry somewhere on board, a fisherman bent over his rod and in the distance the jumble of house fronts, masts and towers, the silhouette of the city. But even more than the life on and around the river, I studied the water itself, which was calm on most of these summer days, inviting, as though made to catch with our oars. I drank it all in and even that early in the day felt a bitter-sweet taste of nostalgia permeate my whole body, while my hands grasped the balustrade of the bridge and behind me the tram passed, cars growled, horses and carts trundled by. I had to tear myself away.

I walked on along the affluent side of the river, past the next bridge and past the club where no flag was waving this early, until I got to the third bridge, which would take me back to my everyday life, leading as it did directly to the bustle of the centre. I crossed, forcing myself not to look left too much, towards the inviting emptiness at the end of the city.

Late in the afternoon, after I had completed my last set of figures, I followed the same route in the opposite direction. The coolness had now given away to a fully saturated splendour of colours, as if it were no longer the wind that ruled the water but the humidity that had evaporated during the day. And I felt the same nostalgia, though sadder now, as if the invitation extended by the water belonged in the past and had lost its validity.

Every day that passes is irreplaceable. That was the message the river gave me. The figures on my desk with their unchanging meaning tried to assert precisely the opposite.

But however much I longed to be rowing again, not once in all those months did I go up the steps to the club. It was not just shyness which prevented me, although I knew full well that there was no place for me among the groups of people that gathered on the balconies and sundecks in the late afternoon. They toasted and clinked glasses, travelled short distances in dinghies with a basket full of delicacies and a parasol. Sometimes a skimpy mast was put up and a sail hoisted above the little clinker-built ships, because effort was not the aim of the sportsmen who frequented the building in these months. They were partying. The main reason for avoiding the club was the feeling that I only had any business there in the company of David and Doktor Schneiderhahn, that somehow I wanted to keep the spot pure until we reassembled to continue the mission that something or someone had given us. Yes, it sounds exalted, but that's how I thought about it at the time.

The evenings were the hardest. I bought a new pair of plimsolls and in them I jogged along the river, out of town, to keep my fitness level up, past all the places we had seen from the water a few weeks earlier. My feet made a slapping sound on the cobbles. Because of the thin soles I could

57

feel every bump. Everything was in blossom. The bushes and the grasses. The cowparsnip, the rape seed, the honeysuckle, the small, plump dandelions. Everything was wide open, drinking in the heavy evening air and in exchange yielding up its scent, its sap, the downy fluff which tried to escape the earth but floated only for a moment in the stillness and then swirled back down into the lush greenery. Now and then I lost sight of the river because of the hedge of fast-growing plants, but all the while I knew it was alongside me, cool and wide, sometimes turning languidly, in the knowledge that it was greater and stronger than all the growth and teeming life along the bank. I missed it, missed the daily intercourse with the water, but the river couldn't care less, it didn't react.

I ran upstream and occasionally, when I got my second wind and my legs wanted to go faster and faster without feeling exhaustion, it went through me like a battle-cry: 'To the source!' Further and further, to where the river began. But I knew very well that there was no source. This river was as slow and stubborn as our country, created by the confluence of two smaller rivers. We had checked it, David and I, on the map that hung in the clubhouse. There was no beginning, it had no origin. It acted as though it had always been here. Sometimes we even doubted if it flowed.

In a quiet spot beyond the last café I'd do exercises to strengthen my arms and shoulders. Then I'd turn round and run back to town. Everything was marvellous, I could see that, but also infinitely sad. The melancholy feeling of the end of the afternoon now gave way to pure pain. I could feel the regular beat of my heart and the pumping of my lungs in my chest. But in that place the feeling of how alone I was that summer, how hopelessly alone, weighed on me more heavily. I wondered where David was now. What business was Schneiderhahn conducting, and in what part of the south? On the terrace of a café by the water's edge a waiter in a long apron was cleaning the tables, cloth in one hand, in the other a bunch of beer mugs. The sun was setting, the last customers were leaving, in a carriage and on bikes. My feet raced over the stones and there were tears in my eyes.

Eyes wide open, I sat on my bed late into the evening. Sounds sometimes wafted in through my bedroom window. Walkers whose steps echoed loudly off the brick walls, a sentence from their conversation. The bell of a tram approaching the depot, and sometimes from the distance a snatch of an indistinct noise that resembled music. The world was full of things happening, and I wasn't part of it. I squeezed my arms, my thighs and my calves to feel if I was getting stronger. I was counting the days until September.

We were there. *Pünktlich.* David still tanned and relaxed as ever. Schneiderhahn with crew-cut hair, which seemed to have lightened under the southern sun, but also with heavier bags under his dark eyes and a face that bore the traces of tough nocturnal negotiations rather than a healthy summer complexion. And I, with the pent-up energy of two months of office work and my heart pounding under my sports shirt, which had been washed and even pressed with razor-sharp creases. My body and his, the boat, our common memory, none of them had forgotten anything. As if it were meant to be, a ray of sunlight skimmed the white roof of the clubhouse and caught us as we pushed off from the raft. As if nothing had happened, we set off towards the bridge, the tall sky, the vastness. Schneiderhahn also seemed to relish the reunion. He gave us no instructions at all. No directions, no exhortations. Out of the corner of my eye I could see him riding along the path by the river on his bike with its white tyres, I saw his gleaming spokes, saw how he had clipped his briefcase to a tube of the frame. Not staring at us as usual or with his eyes focused pensively on the path, but with his head raised cheerfully, looking around, enjoying the late sun and the breeze playing through his quiff, I think, a man who seemed to be forgetting his cares for a moment, letting go of the handlebars with one hand and one finger tucked into his waistcoat, stretching, perhaps humming quietly to himself or trying to whistle a tune. Our oars pumped water away, our backs creaked, whenever we made slightly care-less movements the water splashed and spat in all direc-tions – today it was a festive sound.

Schneiderhahn instructed us to have a quick shower and then to join him in the club. In the tall room with its enor-mous windows looking out on to the water, he had chosen a table in an out-of-the-way corner with a large glass of beer resplendent on it and a pile of papers spread out. He smiled at us. Ordered two glasses of ice-cold lemonade. Banged the papers. They were all intended for us. Somewhere in the midst of his affairs, in a hotel room in Paris or Nice or Sanary, he had covered them with detailed schedules and diagrams. They were his plans for us for a whole year, up to next summer. I looked at them with awe and David too seemed dumbfounded. This was no longer a joke, boating

60

for fun, this was a project that would leave us scarcely any concentration, time or energy for anything else, a task that required absolute dedication. I was ready for it, only too keen. I saw David hesitating. But this time even he, who always had the right, succinct response at his command at the right moment and so was able to turn every situation easily to his own advantage, could not withstand the compelling power of Doktor Alfred Schneiderhahn. Those plans there on the table simply had to be carried out. They couldn't remain just plans and ideals.

Ideals? Yes, somehow it became clear to us that afternoon that Schneiderhahn hadn't become a coach to relax, to get some healthy fresh air in his lungs every day when he had become too old to take to the water himself, if he ever had done so in the past – and to be honest I doubted it. He was a man who was driven, for whom a lot depended on our performance. But what that was, was not clear to me, and even today I can only surmise. Schneiderhahn was not someone for explanations and justifications; the very fact that he occupied himself with us so intensively, that a man who was patently troubled by so many other concerns felt we were important, that the schedules on the table would remain papers covered with meaningless figures without our cooperation – all that meant that we could do nothing but submit ourselves to his authority. And that's what he was counting on.

A movement that is resumed after a period of inactivity is not usually stiff and awkward, but on the contrary surprisingly easy. It is as though a residue of knowledge is present from before the interruption, a little unused credit. Only subsequently, in the second and third training sessions, do the limbs protest, do things refuse to go smoothly and naturally any longer, so that everything has to be co-ordinated and learned afresh. That's how the body's memory works, and that's what happened with us. The effortless first training session was a gift, a joy at the renewed acquaintance. In the weeks and months that followed, we had to toil. Now there seemed to be a different person behind me every day, while I produced different mistakes daily and developed new faults in the movement of an arm or leg. We looked jealously at experienced crews, who in the meantime had also started training again and passed us effortlessly. On Saturdays particularly, it was very busy on the water. The larger boats, fours and eights, didn't worry at all about the waves. Sometimes they challenged each other to a race over a certain stretch, and a little later a triumphant cheer went up from the winners' boat. Schneiderhahn warned us to keep our eyes in our own boat. We could only test ourselves against each other, against our own as yet unfulfilled potential.

The autumn progressed, the wind got stiffer, the waves became higher. Daily we lifted our boat into and out of the water, every day we were soaked by spray and rain. Sometimes I took my jacket off because I reckoned my muscles had become warm to defy the cold. I laid it in front of me in the space under the stretcher, where within a few minutes it became useless. The blue woollen material became black and heavy, saturated with the water which after two or three waves had broken over the side was left in the bottom of the boat and slopped to and fro, to the rhythm of our strokes but in the opposite direction, like a water pendulum beneath our laborious machine. We got wet every day, but not once did that dream of the May day in the rain repeat itself. At best we achieved a kind of stability in our toiling, a heavy hanging and tugging on the oars, a ploughing of the boat with us feeling our muscles harden – and that also gave a kind of satisfaction. I had become a workhorse, a labourer who did his job and carried out the plan under scudding clouds. Occasionally, as I counted off stroke after stroke and nevertheless saw the bank moving past me only slowly and even then joltingly, I saw Schneiderhahn's papers in my mind and realized that for all the laboriousness somewhere a line could be drawn through a figure each time, through a number that had become a reality that we had put behind us. I imagined that we were progressing not just over the water but also through the columns, and that as the days went by, pages became superfluous, having been worked through, and fluttered down, right across the images of our rowing on the river, just as they sometimes do with calendar pages in modern films to indicate that a long period is now passing quickly.

But often there wasn't even the satisfaction that comes after completing a difficult chore. Nothing felt natural. Everything remained imperfect. My feelings of despair were like those in the first few months with the rowdy lads in the eight. I was frightened that David would give up, lose heart and confidence in me. Perhaps it was just coincidence that we had rowed so well together in the summer. It didn't help either that Schneiderhahn suddenly seemed to disapprove of everything that up to now had worked so smoothly between us. The whole mechanism had to be dismantled. Obviously there was not much right with it in his eyes. He made us do exercises that didn't solve those difficulties and snags, but magnified them. The moment that our balance was at its most unstable, as we moved forwards, when we were about to accelerate in order to get a firm grip on the water again, he made us slow down or even insert a pause, during which the oars had to float at right angles to the boat above the water. And it was autumn. There was never calm water to help us in that balancing exercise. *'Langsamer!'* he would yell in annoyance, when we simply wanted to go faster in the boat, and the boat, the weather and the water seemed to be agreeing with us. Faster, past the threadbare reeds and the bare, crooked trees. Faster, past the men in the other boats, with their colourful shirts and their moustaches. Faster, finish the work and back home.

December. Autumn storms gave way to the first hail. When I walked home from the office the water was scarcely visible, like a black no man's land in the paved city. Winter set in early that year. At the beginning of the month the temperature fell to near zero. As if this were a sign, the shopkeepers got their seasonal decorations out of their boxes earlier than usual. Vendors of hot chestnuts and small, useless gifts appeared on street corners.

My office and even David's school did not finish until it was already dark. Only at the weekends could we go on to the icy, grey water. Still we were expected to show up at the club building three times a week. Between the racks on which the boats lay, Schneiderhahn had grouped a small collection of exercise equipment. A table with a rubber mat on it. Cast-iron dumbbells of five and ten kilos. A bar with dark red discs at both ends. A wooden handle around which you had to wind a new white rope with a squat, round weight attached, like those the coalman or the potato merchant used, to strengthen the wrists. Two electric lamps cast a little light in the place where we went through our exercises. The clear sound of metal on metal, occasionally mixed with our groans and sighs, rang eerily through the boathouse, which apart from our corner was completely dark.

For the first time I had a chance to observe David's face when he was exerting himself. Even when he did deep squats with the red discs or lay back and brought the dumbbells in front of his chest and then lowered towards the ground again in an arc, his features remained virtually the same. Perhaps they became a little sharper as he sucked the oxygen into his lungs. And they swelled in his already firm face, though not excessively, when he breathed out and flexed his muscles. I saw the sweat that darkened his shirt collar when I helped him put the bar on his neck. His breath blew into my face when I held his feet and he did his abdominal exercises. So that's how he looks when we row hard, I thought, and tried not to let him notice that I was observing him. I focused my eyes past his shoulders outside the circle of light.

When he held me, he sometimes looked at me with an encouraging smile. Occasionally he said: 'Come on!' We stood opposite each other when we did knee bends, windmills, bunny hops. On the coldest of those evenings we

65

would breathe white clouds in front of us, which mingled and floated away together between the racks, up to the roof beam.

Other oarsmen regarded the cold weather as a boon, a welcome extension of their winter break. The club was only visited to play cards, for meetings or dinners with large carafes of red wine and filling buffets. Sometimes a drinker would come down for a little while, lured by the sounds and light from a quiet part of the building. Some sly comment would be shouted, and David would grin and make a retort that was much wittier.

In the changing-rooms the water had been turned off and so we went straight home after the last exercises. David jumped on to his English bike and shouted a brief farewell as he rode off. I put on my jacket over my thick woollen suit and, holding the collar in one hand, trotted along the quay, over the bridge, down Emerald Street, round the corner, in through our front door. As I spooned up the food that had been kept warm for me on the stove, my wrists and forearms still trembled from the effort. In bed, I pulled the rough blanket high over my stiff shoulders. I quickly fell into a dreamless sleep and woke content but still stiff. There were frost flowers on the windows which the architect had not intended.

Schneiderhahn did not appear during our sessions. Only the first time had he initiated us into the operation of the equipment and given us a clipboard with his instructions on it, again in that curious handwriting and squeezed into sharply demarcated columns. But on one of the last days in the year he suddenly appeared, a silent ambassador who loomed up out of the shadows between the racks and invited us to a 'talk' at his home. We went the following evening.

Home was a hotel on the other side of town, in the vicinity of the central station. The hotel entrance was in a narrow street which had formerly been the entertainment centre for seamen on shore leave and still had a busy, grubby look. There were bars, but also cheese warehouses and a district police station. Its other side looked out over a canal basin, on which two tour boats, unused now in the winter, were moored and across which plied a ferry, specially designed to tempt passengers coming out of the nearby station to make the crossing to the hotel. Even from a distance they could see a modest neon sign: 'Café Restaurant Eden Hotel'.

What a difference there was between the various parts of town. Our brick neighbourhoods. The smart canals. The quays and docks. The districts full of detached houses surrounding the park. And here – where people from the provinces with briefcases and bags, but also international travellers with a porter behind them, arrived in the city, emerging from the exits of the station before fanning out across the broad square and diving into the alleyways and streets of the city – here a hotch-potch of entertainment and commerce prevailed. The messages on the facades changed every year and sometimes every season, they were clad with hanging signs, plastered with posters, daubed with slogans and in the evening covered with hundreds of lamps and lanterns, most of them orange and red. People thronged through the streets until late at night. They ate and drank, the sound of singing or violin music came from the bars. Only the trams had the same blue colour all over town. My father saw to that.

The door of the hotel closed behind us and immediately it was quiet. Thick curtains muffled the street noises, our shoes walked over a soft, springy carpet. At a polished desk sat a friendly night porter, who pointed us to two arm-chairs in which we could wait for our host. David crossed his legs and looked curiously around the long foyer. On a table, arranged in a fan, was a bouquet of newspapers from all the important continental capitals: Paris and London, Prague and Vienna, Budapest and Berlin. But there was Schneiderhahn already, in shirt-sleeves, with his checked jacket slung loosely over his shoulders. He led the way to his room on the second floor, which looked out over the canal basin. On the other side the stream of lights moved steadily between the terminal building and the city.

Doktor Schneiderhahn made a vulnerable impression, here on his home ground. He seemed more timid, although I couldn't have said why that was. He had prepared for our visit, as I assumed he prepared thoroughly for everything. The writing table had been placed in the middle of the room and covered with a checked cloth, on which were placed a pile of books, the largest at the bottom, and a num-ber of papers. There was a litre bottle of beer with a white top and two glasses. An oil lamp stood next to it and cast high shadows into the four corners of the room. Schneider-hahn poured himself a gin, from a round earthenware jug. On a hook against the door of the wardrobe hung the enor-mous winter overcoat with the fur collar, on the floor along the walls and on the windowsill there were books, writing equipment and piles of newspapers. Until then I had always assumed that the business he was engaged in related to import and export, to the world of high finance of which the calculations that I carried out in the office were the ultimate consequence and the inanimate object. But the quantity of books in this room and their appearance contradicted that notion. There were distinguished bindings with gold print on them and new editions with elegant dust jackets, the titles of which were difficult to read. 'Sütterlin,' I said to myself. But I also saw brochures printed in sharply contrasting colours with the sanserif letters of our brick neighbourhood and of the revolution. I could read the titles of those, but they meant nothing to me.

Schneiderhahn surveyed our progress during the nearly twelve months that we'd known each other. As he went through month by month, the leaves of my film calendar occurred to me again and the lists of figures came to life. All of this wasn't enough, I understood Schneiderhahn to be saying. A proper build-up had to lead somewhere. He took two books off the top of the pile, put them on one side and pushed the one underneath towards us to look at. He poured himself another glass and leaned back. The book was bound in dark-blue cloth and was decorated with the picture of a large bell in black and gold. It was the peace bell which had summoned the young people of all nations to Berlin two years ago. I turned the pages carefully, David leaned forward towards me and, with his cheek close to mine, looked at the report of the Games. The text was strewn with illustrations in soft pastel colours, small-sized, the kind that they gave away free with certain kinds of tobacco. Someone – Schneiderhahn himself? – had had to smoke an awful lot to complete the collection. The pictures were mainly of grinning sportsmen after their victories, hair just combed, eyes retouched in radiant blue. Occasionally the camera had also captured them during their performances – horse and rider floating over a fence, a swimmer with his arm raised above the foam. The swimmers from our country had done well; we saw a picture of their female trainer, who in her ample dress looked like the Queen. We saw the awesome black athletes who ran faster than ordinary human beings and for that reason were always cheerful. And our countryman, the fastest white man in the world, who had lost only to the two black Americans in the hundred metres.

Schneiderhahn put out a hand and leafed through to the end of the book, where there was a report on the rowing. With a loving gesture he smoothed the paper at the picture of a coxless pair. The boat, or at least that portion of it that fitted into the small rectangle of the cigarette card, lay diagonally in smooth blue water. The oarsmen had stretched their arms in front of them in an unnatural pose, which did, however, show their broad shoulders off to good advantage, horizontally on the paper, and with it the broad red line with a golden emblem in the middle which ran across their improbably white shirts at chest height. Their mouths too formed small horizontal strips, not quite smiling but full of manly determination. The front man was slightly slimmer than his comrade. Both of them had lank hair and were looking away from the page, out of the book, at something important in the distance.

'Silver medal,' said Schneiderhahn.

I saw David's finger moving over the page and stopping at the report of the result.

'Were you there?' I asked.

'No, I wasn't there,' said Schneiderhahn in surprise, almost taken aback. I immediately regretted my blunt question, but he didn't seem to hold it against me. He stared past us, diagonally upwards to where the shadows stretched onto the ceiling and against the curtains in the flicker of the lamp.

For the first time since we had met him I managed to see his face at really close range. Beneath the bristly hair, grey with a hint of dirty blond streaks, was a broad forehead, marked by grooves and bumps. It may have been because of the oil lamp that lit the Doktor's face from below, but the rest of his face too was a landscape of dark pits and fleshy hills. Heavy bags protected the deep-set, bright blue eyes. Large pores and burst blood vessels covered the turnip-shaped nose. Enormous ears framed his portrait, only one part of which didn't seem to have been marked by a hard life; the thin mouth, pink and delicately shaped like that of a baby, innocent and sad at the same time.

'Perhaps next time,' said David in an attempt to close the subject.

Schneiderhahn now looked at us penetratingly. Then he smiled. 'Do you two know where the next Games are going to be held?'

'Tokyo,' said David.

'Then I won't be there again. Maybe I don't need to be there.' Schneiderhahn paused. 'But what about you, lads?'

71

David raised an eyebrow. I looked at our host in disbelief. In the year that I had known him, I had never heard him make a joke. But did I know him? I knew nothing about Schneiderhahn. Nothing about his business, nothing about his trips, nothing about the books along the walls in this respectable but not particularly luxurious hotel. And I still didn't know why he had picked us out and why he had spent so much time and effort on us. It didn't occur to me to ask him, nor did he give us any chance that evening. As though nothing had been said about the previous topic, our host slammed the blue book shut in front of our noses and put it aside. He poured himself another drink. We were given the rest of the sweet beer, he had another gin. Now two other books were put on the table. They had soft covers and contained illustrated treatises on physical preparation and rowing technique. Schneiderhahn read aloud to us from his papers. The first sheet that he had written on contained the competition fixture list for the following year. And below it were the cyclical plans that he had developed to prepare us for those races.

'Planning is the foundation of every mechanical movement,' he lectured. 'Success can be planned.'

'But surely luck can't,' objected David. 'You don't know how strong your opponents are going to be.'

'You can eliminate as many factors as possible that get in the way of luck. In any case, what's left is not resistant to luck.'

Schneiderhahn said it with conviction and even a certain enthusiasm, and that enthusiasm communicated itself to us. In an almost comradely tone we went on talking about

races and plans, about the condition of our boat and ourselves, about the number of hours that we could make
available to prepare ourselves. Schneiderhahn ordered a
second bottle of beer to be brought up to the room – 'the last
one, until the summer,' he said as he did so. The comradely
tone of three men around a lamp in a room by a dark canal,
three men with a common purpose, that atmosphere of
almost unforced togetherness, never existed again between
the three of us. It was impossible, we were too different
from each other for that and there was also too much difference in what we did. But something of what was created
that evening was preserved in the following months, an
understanding, a realization that we couldn't quite fathom
ourselves but that was as good as a treaty with a text written out in scores of sections.

'Well,' observed David when we got outside. And I understood him. I had the two instruction manuals under my arm.

'Come on,' he called a little later, when we were on the
other side of the water, and with those words he broke into a
wild sprint for a tram which had just left. I ran behind him,
suddenly rejoicing inwardly, past the stripes and flashes of a
cold but not yet sleeping city. A little later, I stood next to
him, gasping for breath, on the rear balcony of the tram,
which swung round a corner squeaking and rattling. I
looked into the tram, where groups of people sat without
speaking to each other. Soft bodies. Sleepy faces on their way
home. The tram rang its bell. I was reminded of my father
and of the depot into which the tram would drive in the not
too distant future, to stand all night long in a darkness that
stank of oil and wet clothes. Then I thought of myself,

against a painted blue sky and with unnaturally blond hair, as a picture given away free with a purchase of tobacco.

Spring had not yet begun when we competed in our first race. The planking in front of the club was wet with rain and a fierce wind drove inky black clouds across the sky. Nevertheless the race director had considered the conditions good enough to allow the club's internal competition to take place. Cursing and swearing, the teams took to the water – but that was for form's sake, because there was also something manly about going out in the wind and the rain, while their safe return was certain. The river might rage and howl, but it wasn't the Bering Sea, or the Straits of Magellan. For the last few weeks the coach had made his exercises a little easier, to allow us to regain our natural rhythm. And the intensity gradually returned. Longer days, shorter strokes. Or were we wrong, and was it not the exercise material, but we ourselves that had changed? Had we acquired a solidity during those long winter months, evenings under the dumbbells, Saturday afternoons and Sunday mornings on the water, that we had not had before?

Not until a week before our first race did Schneiderhahn explain to us how to start. Blades in the water, edges just below the surface, boat balanced, ready to draw immediately after the off was given. Calmly. Hard and long, but calm, that was how the first stroke must be rowed. Then two three-quarter-length strokes, to pick up speed. Then another full stroke, followed by twenty extra-hard strokes and by that time you should be in the race, your own race – you didn't let others determine your build-up. 'Eyes in the boat. Don't keep looking at your opponents. Control. *Diszi-plin*. Think of your own planning.'

If he was nervous when we took to the water, he didn't show it. I was, my heart was in my mouth. I also felt slightly giggly, out of place. The other crews were made up of experienced oarsmen. They were older, wore expensive kit, they had moustaches and a few were even sporting roguish caps. I could imagine what was going to happen: in a few minutes, half an hour at most, it would be obvious that we were not in the same class; they would not only go faster but would do so in a completely natural way, smiling pityingly at us and, who knows, even shouting encouragement to each other during the race. For all those months that we had been training for ourselves, we could pull the wool over our eyes. There was nothing outside ourselves to measure our performance against, no one to compare ourselves with, no one to judge us. Except Schneiderhahn. But who was he? A lonely figure in a ridiculous rain cape and wellingtons who watched us leave the landing stage. A foreigner. I wished we were back training. I longed for the sense of aloneness on the water, for the cosy circle of light as we worked with the dumbbells in the boathouse.

Nothing went the way we had practised it, everything we'd agreed was flouted. Even at the gun, during the first long stroke, a shudder went through the boat and my blade did not clear the water. Immediately we were askew, but instead of calming things down by continuing to go slowly, my next stroke was even more hurried and uncontrolled, so that David had to correct it forcibly, and from the shore our boat must have looked like a drunken duck, its stupid feet entangled in waterweeds and strands of plants, making furious attempts to take off. I tried to repeat to myself the instructions that I'd been through a thousand times, but my thoughts couldn't keep pace with my actions. My body was still a step ahead of my brain, it had taken over command from me and was plunging into the race with crazy, unfocused energy. Out of the corner of my eye I saw not a supple catch and finish but fountains that splashed whenever we chopped the blade into the waves. To my horror I also realized that I had forgotten to keep count and so began counting the hard twenty at an arbitrary point, and added ten, and another ten, as a kind of self-punishment to chastise our mindless power. Only then did I look up.

We were alone.

The crews that had started to the left and right of us were already almost two lengths behind. I could see the backs of the rowers but also the eagerly bobbing front edges of their bows. And as an astonished calm descended on me, I saw how the distance between them and us increased with every stroke.

We crossed the finish line with a comfortable lead. Not for a moment had our rowing resembled what we had practised. The race dictated its own style and its own laws that were not transmitted by the head but processed directly by the body. I realized from my wild panting that we had rowed at an unusually high tempo. At the same time my arms and legs felt as if they had not done enough. Schneiderhahn grabbed David's blade and pulled us to the side. 'Gratuliere!' he said. But he wasted no words on the manner in which we had gained our victory.

During the prize ceremony in the clubhouse I noticed that people were looking at us with astonishment and also with respect. It wasn't a wholly pleasant feeling. The victory had not meant that we were accepted into the group of oarsmen, but rather confirmed our status as exceptions. That didn't bother David, he joked with the club members that he knew, and if need be with strangers, just as he had done before that afternoon. If we had lost miserably, he would have behaved in exactly the same way. I scanned the busy room for Doktor Schneiderhahn. He stood right at the back, next to one of the trophy cabinets, glass of cognac in hand. He, I realized properly only now, was an outsider too. Someone who had lost his way, like me.

III

Silence. Behind me I can no longer hear the woodwork creaking. I can now only feel the cold in my feet and fingertips. Am I imagining things, or has the river stopped moving?

There is a moment, there must be a moment just before the water reaches freezing point when it no longer flows but is still liquid. A fraction of a second before the first ice crystal forms and with an inaudible crack continues into space, dividing, reflecting, duplicating, spreading like wildfire in all the variations arithmetic allows, to every corner of the body of water, which freezes into a wonderful pattern, an icy grimace, foam and air bubbles included. But just before that happens, I imagine, there is an instant of stillness in the rising water. The stillness before everything stops. That is how the stillness feels right now.

There is something else. A story David once told me. The ancient Greeks, he said, believed that everything in the universe had previously been connected. One in absolute harmony. Motionlessness. The silence must have been ear-splitting. Then, one day – so were there days back then? – that harmony was disrupted and the world disintegrated with a huge bang. Everything split in two. Since then separate halves have been floating around in space that fit each other exactly and are searching for each other but cannot find their counterpart. Only very occasionally, through one crazy coincidence in millions of encounters, do those two matching halves meet again. There must be a wild convulsion when that happens, a moment of ecstasy so great that time stands still again. Sometimes I think David and I were two of those searching particles.

But I don't even know if I've remembered the story correctly or whether looking for your other half has anything to do with physics or with sport. Perhaps it's just love. But at least I know now that you can train perfectly well for love, and for happiness. I had discovered that you must dare to inflict pain on yourself in order to reach the moment where the opposite poles unite. If that doesn't happen, and usually it doesn't, there's only pain. And a scant consolation: at least you feel you're alive.

Silence. As before the start of a big race. The murmur of the spectators is hushed. The sun is high in the sky. You've raised your hand to the umpire, because your boat is still not properly in its lane. But now it's really positioned right. Parallel with the other boats, centrally between the buoys. You've trailed your fingers through the water and splashed some moisture on your seat to make sure that you don't slide off it in a little while. You suppress the inclination to bring a sip of water to your dry lips. You've dried your fingers again carefully to be able to keep a grip on the oar. You've turned the wing nuts on the stretcher, on the gate of the rigger. Everything is tight. The sun is beating down. On your hands and fingers, which again grasp the wood of the oar tight. On your shoulders, which you've brought close to your knees. You twist your hips carefully to keep the boat balanced, the boat turns with you and behind you you feel another pair of hips moving. All the strength suddenly flows out of you. In the middle of your limp body a hole has appeared where a moment ago your stomach was. You haven't slept and your bowels have emptied themselves twice or three times that morning until it hurt and now they're filled with nothing but sun and fear. You'd like only one thing: to get away from here. But not straight ahead, into the race. No, away, as in: disappear. If necessary into the pit of that stomach of yours filled with sun and fear. So even the sun can hold its breath. If you get out of this alive, if you reach the finish, it'll be the last time you do it, the very last time. What are you frightened of? Not of the opposition, not of the other boats. The fear is about your own plan, the task of surpassing yourself, of reaching deeper and further than you think you can, in order to inflict pain on yourself. You're frightened to live.

In the silence the red flag falls and the 'Off!' sounds and you're away before you realize. Again, your body takes you with it before your head can follow. Spectators leap on to their bikes, there is a noise, you feel your legs pushing off against the stretcher and the water splashing on to your skin. The sun is back in its place, high in the sky. You count the strokes and know that each stroke is irreplaceable and you wouldn't want it to be any other way; before you can think, the next one is already there and many after that.

We won. We also won the first real race, against other crews, from other clubs, with shirts in different colours, stripes oblique or vertical, emblems, waving flags on the bank, we won that too. The setting was a country rowing course on another river, not completely straight, slightly narrower, not that far from our town. The boats which had been brought from all over the country on flat-bottomed barges were laid on improvised racks and supports in a meadow. We walked cautiously down to the water so as not to sprain our ankles or step into cowpats. The finishing line was monitored from an old hotel, which had been completely taken over by volunteers from the organization. Guys in colourful jackets – red, light blue, green and yellow – were handing each other beer in tankards and bottles. They ran to the water's edge and sang when a team in the same colours had won. Dishes of cold meats and salads were passed by waitresses flushed with effort. Here and there piles of dirty plates clattered. There were heated discussions about obstructing your opponents when a boat went beyond the buoys, about changes in the order of the programme. Bespectacled students sat at typewriters and wrote lists of results or announcements from the race directors, who were accommodated on the first floor of the low building. The directors consisted of older gentlemen in dark-blue blazers and grey suits who were addressed with respect by the students and who rewarded that adoration by occasionally treating them as equals. They would tell a joke, they would accept a roll they were offered. They inquired what it was like in the student club these days and in the lecture rooms. At the end of the afternoon collars were even loosened. Two thick-set gentlemen with snow-white hair had taken off their jackets. Fathers on vacation.

81

But the joviality existed only by the grace of the deep seriousness with which the organization had been handled and the rules were observed. That was how one was also expected to view the prizes awarded to the winners. Looked at objectively, the medals were worthless pieces of metal. You could call them 'bits of tin', but 'getting a bit of tin' was something which people talked about only with respect, or with an even more serious variant of it, professed nonchalance. For some events there was even a rotating trophy, a silver-plated cup with delicately worked handles, a pair of crossed oars in the same material on a bed of faded velvet, a bronze sculpture which you could scarcely lift – and we hit upon the last alternative.

Our prize was not a statue but a whole group of statues, because around the figure of Neptune, the God of the Sea, rising with his trident and beard from among the bronze waves, there were also fishes, waving plants and the smiling faces of three water nymphs, all sculpted in the same deep brown, gleaming material. I had no problem in finding it marvellous and I am sure that David was as proud of it as I was, but he said 'glorified kitsch' and didn't bother to look at the thing, which was displayed among the other prizes in the restaurant on a table covered with a Persian rug. I, though, let my hand run over the cool material and in the course of the afternoon walked past it a couple more times so that I could enjoy it out of the corner of my eye. I know that the secret of success often consists of making the inevitable seem natural. But I couldn't do it then and now, when I may have mastered the art, I no longer want to do it.

What had we had to do in order to win the prize? Early

in the morning we had won the heat without much trouble. Schneiderhahn had set us the task of concentrating on starting in a controlled way. Not only the winners of the two heats but also the fastest runners-up would get into the final so that half of all the crews taking part would go through. In addition David would have to look over his shoulder a lot that day to steer round the bend without going outside the assigned lane, which was marked with flags and buoys. And we could trust in our preparation, in the fast spring and the solid winter.

This time I followed the instructions so well that it was hard for me to realize after the initial strokes that we were actually involved in a race. My head was unusually clear and registered every component of our movement and the movement of the crew next to us, two heavily built guys wearing orange shirts, naval cadets, who did their very best in a jolting rhythm with both of them coming far out of the vertical at the end of the stroke, so they looked like a pair of scissors opening and closing. I also registered the fact that they still kept pace with us pretty well in that ugly style and when that got through to me I gradually increased the power and tempo, which helped us to pull away from them easily. David steered perfectly past the pickets. I can't even remember the other opponents.

Before the final, in the afternoon, I was more nervous. It was as though Schneiderhahn's suggestions only worked for a limited time. On the results board I saw that we had recorded the fastest time that morning. Then I had seen the statue of Neptune on the Persian rug. As we lay at the start and the umpire shouted instructions to keep the bows of the boats in one line, I suddenly realized that the other two pairs had probably done exactly the same as us. They had, of course, rowed without getting really tired. With our fast time, we had been careless enough to betray our strength. The heats didn't really count. I was so absorbed by this ominous thought that I scarcely heard the starting command and didn't, as was the intention, time my first stroke to coincide with the starting gun but reacted in a very delayed way, after the sound had rung out and the noise of the other boats started up next to me. Or rather behind me, because the curve in the course had been compensated for by having a staggered finish line and this time we had drawn the inside lane so that we had to start with our opponents a few metres ahead of us.

I had intended to catch them before the start of the bend. Then I would see them the moment we had an advantage. But for the first hundred metres it didn't look as though I would manage to do that. In my panic I had followed up my delayed reaction with a frenzied continuation: the rollers under my seat flew forward, leaving me scarcely any time to prepare my back and shoulders for the stroke. David, who never made any comments, snapped angrily, 'Calm down, for God's sake. Use your head!' I felt shame coursing through me. If even David lost confidence in me, how was I to get my arms and legs to listen to me? With the courage of despair I recovered, and when a little later David said, 'Yes, keep it like that', something of the feeling of that morning returned. As we entered the bend, actually more of a curve, I saw to my right first the rudder, then the canvas and then the stroke of one of the other teams, a fat lad with a bright red face, who glanced to the side with an angry look. Perhaps the heat hadn't been a mistake. Immediately afterwards we passed the second team and in the final stretch, where the flat-bottomed barges were moored along the bank and a stand had been improvised, there were cheers and applause as we headed for the finish. 'And now a nice run-in,' said David between two breaths. I tried to lengthen the stroke. With each stroke we increased the distance from the other boats. The applause and cheering increased in volume until it surrounded us completely. The sound of a horn marked the finish. 'Congratulations,' panted David.

The sun was already low in the sky when we unscrewed the riggers in the meadow and tied them together, labelling them with the name of the boat for transport. On the barges by the bank the exuberant mood had given way to another kind of jollity, tired and a little teasing, and the assistants who grabbed the bare hull of our boat looked temperamental after a day of eating bacon and drinking brandy. They would be sailing all night in order to deliver the first material at the boathouses the following morning. As we packed our things, someone would sometimes pass and shout congratulations or a compliment. I felt completely happy. David demonstrated how you could tie an ingenious knot. Two students in light-blue jackets stopped near us.

'Well done, chaps!'

David thanked them, I nodded. Then they asked where we were thinking of studying the following year. David answered, and I froze in mid-movement.

'A good choice, old boy. We'll see you in our first-year eight,' said the first jacket.

'And then in the senior four, I hope,' said the second.

'Both of you!' shouted the first speaker over his shoulder as he walked off, just to be pleasant. Then they put their arms round each other's light-blue shoulders and made a beeline for one of the buffets next to the restaurant.

I looked at David. 'Are you leaving?' I asked cautiously. 'Moving?' I was almost choking. For the first time it became clear to me that for David our adventure might be nothing more than an episode, a small chapter in the rich life which still in large part lay ahead of him. Something that he would soon forget about and would laugh about later, while I couldn't imagine that anything important would happen after this.

'I'm not at all sure yet. I'm certainly going to study at any rate. But where? No idea. I won't decide until the last moment.'

'But what about Tokyo?' I wanted the question to sound like a joke, although I wasn't at all cheerful. If I'd wanted to be serious, then I'd have asked, 'But what about Schneider-hahn?'

'Helsinki. Finland,' said David.

'Finland?'

'The Olympic Committee has made a new decision. The Games won't be held in Tokyo but in Helsinki. If they're held at all. Don't you know what's going on in the world? Don't you read the papers?'

I didn't read the papers. They weren't part of the household where I grew up and not even of the street where that house-hold was, of the people who lived there, or of their lives and deaths that were not mentioned in them anyway. It had nothing to do with poverty or ignorance, but rather with conditioning and tradition. It was simply a different space and time in which we lived, a different year, perhaps a different century. Other events attracted attention there than those in David's world, or Schneiderhahn's. It was odd that all those different worlds with their own chronologies and their own printed matter should co-exist in one town and that you could point them out on the map. In the gemstone district, folders were delivered, bills, reminders from the council. Their content could not be contradicted, any more than could the names carved in stone on the house fronts. In the quiet streets where David lived, the evening paper was delivered to every house to help the digestion. Of course, there were papers on sale near the station which contradicted and started fighting each other on the very first page. From the early morning onwards newspaper sellers stood praising their content and the orderly fan on the low table in the Eden Hotel was nothing more than that, the temporary order in a world which was busy packing its bags, in the process of leaving, ready to go and never return, nothing more than the artificial order of the hotel.

Only the trams were the same in all parts of the city, they linked all those worlds together, and when the trams rolled into the depot after midnight the cleaners and supervisors quite often found a discarded newspaper among the seats, crumpled and lonely, without getting into conversation or alarming anyone. I am sure that my father did not regard such a piece of paper as a message from another world which he might have wanted to get to know about from curiosity, for example. For him, it was rubbish: an object that might have been useful somewhere else, but in his surroundings had no meaning at all and hence had to be cleared away as soon as possible. In our home it wasn't 1939, but simply a year of work, one of many on the way to the last stop, and beyond that last stop lay the unknown eternity, which we didn't trouble our heads about. We knew exactly what the following and the previous stop were called, but nothing about the route on a different line.

There was a time when I felt guilty and insecure about my lack of knowledge. Should I immerse myself in world history, politics, the needs of society? That time is long since past. In my world that summer, water was the most important thing and now I could not imagine what was actually wrong with that. What else should I concern myself with? Was Schneiderhahn so happy then? Did I envy the bosses at my office? Did I want to become a deputy manager? A mayor? An architect? Was there any reason to spread my attention over the rest of the world if I was happy here and now?

There wasn't – and perhaps that was precisely why I realized that as summer approached my interest in the rest of the city began to awaken. Not because the river, the boathouse and David were no longer enough for me, but precisely because I was so full of them that I would have liked to embrace everything without thinking too much. Does a flower open because it lacks something? No, it shows the depths of its soul because it's so full of itself that otherwise it would burst.

There was a morning in spring when I woke at first light and left the house earlier than usual, just to be able to walk along the water's edge and see the rest of the world awaken. I stopped on the bridges as before, but I also walked along one of the wide access roads into town, between the tram rails, in the middle of the street. Everything around me was so unusually clear, etched with such razor-sharpness, the houses, the leaves on the trees, the cobbles in the street – as if the finest master of realism had painted his masterpiece. If it had not been so beautiful, it would have hurt my eyes. I stretched, full length, and let loose a wild, strange cry.

In the distance I heard a horse's hooves scraping between the houses and the rattle of milk churns that was echoed by the house fronts. The sound was like music. I felt like saying good morning to everyone. But there wasn't anyone, so I said good morning to animals and inanimate things. A bird, a wonderful red postbox, a cat crossing the road. I revelled in the morning and the city and at the same moment wanted it to be afternoon already so we could take to the water and again row away from town.

Another day found me in the early evening, with tired limbs after the training session, on the balcony of a tram that was brushing past the terraces of houses and throngs of people on the way to the station, which was gleaming in the late sunlight with its red-brick front and its decorations like those of a cathedral. I had wanted to shout something to the people, but didn't know what. They looked so beautiful and so pleased with themselves and with walking through the town.

A little later I saw the sun go down from the ferry that sails from behind the station across the great expanse of water to the docks and warehouses. I imagined I could smell the sea air. I'd never been here before and had no business here; I stood by the railing when the deck emptied and went back immediately. I threw my head back and sniffed again. Beneath me, I felt the deck moving up and down; behind me, the engine pounded, the funnel spewed white clouds. I felt at home. The city gradually became mine and I became part of the whole city.

If there was something else besides pure happiness that took me into town on those evenings, it might have been uncertainty about its durability. The possibility of David's leaving in the autumn still preyed on my mind. I hadn't forgotten his remark, although I did my best not to think about it.

Summer began early that year and, though we didn't know it yet, was to last an infinity. On one of the first warm days, a Sunday, my reconnoitring took me in the direction of his house. I knew where it was, in a street by the park, close to one of the richly decorated entrances, and I'd noted down the number of the house. The fine weather had lured the inhabitants of the town into the park and they were still there now, as evening fell, in large numbers. No longer as they had been earlier in the day, amusing themselves exuberantly, pushing each other and commenting excitedly, as though the sun were a special offer, an exceptional bargain in the sales that would never be repeated. By now, the mood on the paths had become sedate. People were still walking around enjoying themselves, but through it all a deep weariness was also perceptible. Walking sticks tapped. There was the crunch of a pram. Voices were

hushed. It had been almost too much, a day off and marvellous weather into the bargain. A brass band played
waltzes under a white dome and now even the waltzes
seemed tired and sluggish.

I entered the park on the eastern side, close to a tram stop,
and hesitated to leave it again. I thought that the light would
stay longer in the wide avenues outside than here under the
dark-green leaves. I sought out the tall trees, avoided the
open lawns and meadows, walking along the edges of the
park. Only when I saw the lamps lighting up did I walk outside again and then I was immediately in the street where
David lived. No more than a few metres from his house.

All the houses here were tall and imposing. Those on the
park side were also wide, with verandas and wooden
extensions, and some even had little fairy-tale towers. On
the other side of the street, however, the houses formed a
closed front and had grey steps and white ornaments. They
differed from each other in those ornaments: sometimes
they were statues holding up a balcony, sometimes
tableaux of tiles containing a reference to the profession of
the resident, but the houses also showed in the way in
which the bricks were joined that they were there in the first
instance for their own benefit and for that of their residents,
not to serve a greater whole. Often two or three were built
in the same manner, but undoubtedly not because the
design of the street required it. It was rather as if in their
occasional uniformity they were giving a polite nod to each
other or offering a small token of respect. Those who lived
here did so because this dignity suited them like a coat
designed especially for them. And just as happens with

good clothes, the dignity of the buildings reflected on the residents. That was how you achieved harmony – not through forced uniformity, but through an intimate embrace of differences. In all its variety, this street seemed to have a greater unity than ours, where you couldn't guess who belonged behind which house front. Where it didn't matter.

In the monumental villas which adjoined the park, the lamps had already been lit. I walked further into the street. The light hadn't lasted longer there than in the park, but the heat had. The stones retained it better than the grass and the trees. The grey granite of the steps and doorways especially still glowed with the heat. A church bell rang. I looked up at the spires. It was half past eight. I stopped opposite David's house, under the overhanging branches of a large tree. Anyone looking out of the windows of the first floor in the summer would scarcely realize that they lived in town, the covering of foliage was so thick and extensive. The windows of the house were mirror-smooth and dark. I tried to imagine what the rooms looked like. The lamps, the paintings in their sparkling frames on the walls, the gleaming tables and the comfortable chairs and sofas on their islands of Persian carpet. The stairwell with its thick red carpet and yet the echo of marble floors and tall white walls. The garden behind the house on to which David's bedroom would look out, with gravel paths, box hedges, large roses and white hydrangeas at the corners, and at the back perhaps, yes almost certainly, a green summerhouse with a slate roof, for the pleasure and amusement of his elder sister. Those born here had no need to fear anything.

I crossed the street and laid a hand on the warm, worn stone of the small flight of steps leading to the front door. Three steps, he went up and down those every evening and every morning. I looked at the shiny, polished nameplate and the brass bell pull, the flap for talking to unknown tradesmen; through the grating of the door I actually caught a glimpse of white marble in the hall. Then, standing close to the house, I looked straight up along the front past the sea gods which bore the balcony, past the tall windows on the first floor and two floors higher, past the white hoisting beam at the top. I felt dizzy, it was as though the front of the house was starting to move, or it was suddenly a street, a long road that was wobbling, a wall that was leaning forwards and would collapse on me. I bent my neck even further back and saw the evening sky, the horizon with the beginnings of moonlight and a few white clouds, and in them I regained my balance. Then I turned round and began moving, walking, no, running away from the house, across the street, through the gate into the park, where it was now almost completely dark.

There were scarcely any people left, but I still made sure that I stayed outside the range of the lamps. Tyres still occasionally zoomed along the bicycle path, preceded by a small lamp. I slowed down. My breathing gradually became more regular. I walked across the sand of a bridle path that was enclosed by bushes and tried to gather my thoughts again. Thoughts about David, myself, his place in the town, the strange life on the water that we shared.

Suddenly a group of riders came towards me out of the shadows, the sound of their hooves muffled by the soft ground. Three or four horses in a languid gallop, on their way to the stables. Their enormous bodies brushed past me on either side; it was too late to jump clear. Flanks, bridles, creaking leather. I smelled their warm sweat, the odour of manure and earth. Someone swore and told me I should watch where I was going. It sounded muffled among the tall bushes, as if we were under water, and the movements of the horses seemed to be slowed down too. Then a ray of light fell on the blonde hair and the face of a girl. In a flash I saw her narrow nose, broad mouth, and hair which rolled back from her forehead and disappeared behind her face like a crown of rays.

That night I dreamed that I felt a small, narrow body next to mine. I hugged it to me so that my hips covered hers. Her small, firm breasts lay high against my chest. Judith? Jet? Jennie? Jessica? Jolanda? I had forgotten the name of David's sister.

I, who never dreamed. From my earliest childhood I'd known nothing except deep, dreamless sleep. In fact, sleep began at the moment that I put my hand under the tightly tucked-in blanket, felt the cool sheet and pulled the corner of the covers from the bed. As if you were opening a door. I liked keeping the fold as small as possible and sliding under the covers as if I were slipping into an envelope. Mail with an unknown destination, returned to sender at the same address the following morning. As soon as I was under the covers and felt the bed around me on all sides, I sank into sleep. No sleepless hours, not even any last thoughts. The night was a different room, a separate space, where nothing

94

happened that should happen elsewhere. Bedroom, dining-room. Hall, bathhouse. Street and river. Club, office.

But in these months all that began to change. The boundaries were blurred, the sluice gates opened. I sat in the office and thought of the water. As I copied columns into the ledger, the figures changed under my hands into hard strokes, soft strokes, a *fartlek* that threatened to wriggle its way off the paper, out of the door, towards the open air, to the river. I sat with my mother at the round dining-table and as I looked at her I saw another face, the ingrained line of worry and fear around the corner of her mouth gave way to a kindly smile full of confidence. I ate the meal she had made for me, but tasted something else. I looked at the tram rails along the quay and saw not the firm tracks but the glimmer of scores of possibilities, destinations in every corner of the city. And when I lay in bed in the evenings, I listened for a long time to the sounds of the house and the city, and I also heard sounds that weren't there, the splashing of water, a clear voice ringing in a marble stairwell, the sound of horses' hooves on a dark path.

I dreamed. Objects and people acquired a new face. Actions which I performed every day changed their meaning. Something had shifted. I couldn't explain it to myself, but it felt as if things had gained a new charge that was fuller and richer and hence truer. It was not as though a new light were being shed on things, it was more as if things themselves were beginning to radiate, as though the light came from within and revealed their true nature.

There was one afternoon after training when I was sitting on one of the benches in the changing-room, my head in my hands, my wet clothes thrown into a corner, buttocks on the rough wood. Too tired even to see the tiles between my feet. I heard only the rushing of the jet of water under which David was rinsing himself off, first a long way away, then closer, as if he were approaching together with the shower. I raised my head and supported it in my hands. In a mist of water and steam I saw David standing there.

The black curls across his forehead and down past his ears through which the water was trickling. His eyebrows, his broad forehead and heavy chin, the thick lips. His proud nose with the eyes on either side that always looked ironic, except now, in this unreal moment between day and dream. His shoulders and the shadow of the muscles on his chest and in his arms. His belly, not flat but with a slight curve – he would grow fat when he stopped training and he would laugh about it, it wouldn't matter to him at all. Sturdy legs, with muscles like shields at the front, and between his belly and legs, still full of lather, with a wreath of black hair that continued in a strip upwards, almost to his chest, his dark sex with the pink tip.

David was, I thought, exactly as David should be. You couldn't put it in any other way. Everything he had I would have liked to possess too. He stretched and looked at me. Winked. 'Come on!'

Laboriously, suddenly very aware of my gawky body with its long tough muscles, I stood up. Hadn't I seen him properly before?

He made room for me. We almost touched each other. From close to I saw the tiny black hairs on his skin.

Of course I'd never seen him properly. He sat behind me. All those hours on the water I could only feel him and then only he had the task of occasionally looking round and steering our boat. We rowed forwards, but with our backs to the direction in which we were going. I tried not to think about the future at all, but I wasn't very good at it yet.

We won. Between rain showers, on a lake where the finish was the imaginary line between two small boats.

On a still pond between the villas of an ancient town, cheered on by the dignitaries, their wives and children. Probably maids, too.

In a borrowed boat, carefully checked over by Doktor Schneiderhahn, on a long straight canal with only the occasional flagpole, in one of the northern provinces.

And on the new rowing course in the newly planted woods on the southern edge of the city. Schneiderhahn had taken us there with him two days before the race to get us used to the wind and the flow of the water in front of empty stands; this was different for each of the six boats that could start side by side, or so he said.

After each victory there was a raft of honour, usually an improvised jetty at which we tied up to applause and where a chairman or a race director or a mayor walked carefully up to us – the raft tipping, water lapping the gleaming polished shoes – and presented the medals.

Our sweaty faces beneath dishevelled hair. Sweat only really starts to flow after the race. A handshake and a medal. 'Good race!' 'Yes, thank you very much.' Immediately after the finish David has already said 'Congratulations' drily. It becomes a habit. Schneiderhahn keeps in the background. Looks on from a distance, bicycle in hand. Laughter when a wave lifts the raft upwards, so that it strikes the rigger and almost capsizes us. Doesn't matter. You allow yourself to be pushed off by half a dozen willing hands, blades go under water and we row off calmly. Together now, while the applause swells again, letting them see why we won. Power and technique. Catching the water smoothly, although it doesn't matter now. I wonder what David is looking like? Only after we get out, in the boat area, do we have trembling knees. A taste of blood in the mouth. An annoying cough that goes on for an hour. 'Rower's cough,' says David. He's heard that expression from older oarsmen. He really does know everything. Everything goes right this summer.

With each new achievement, our esteem grew in the club. At least I assume so, because the indications were scarcely perceptible. When we took our boat out and rowed away to start a training session, a few more people looked at us for just a little longer. When we rigged our boat up for a race, there were always a few interested spectators around. I assumed that people talked about us with a kind of appreciation. We gained results for the club, and trophies. But someone who is respected doesn't necessarily belong. Nothing about my position in the scheme of things, or my feelings, changed. I still regarded myself as a guest in high society, as an outsider who rowed along with the rowers, not part of the tightly knit group of people who belonged in the changing-rooms, at the bar and on the terraces, and who could recognize each other effortlessly elsewhere in town too, for whom just a word was enough in a language which distinguished them from other people, even outside the club.

And I cared less and less. I was concerned only with myself, and with David. With who we were together. And with Schneiderhahn of course, who – if I had been aware of it – gave a shining example of independence. It was no accident that he didn't congratulate us on the raft of honour but only later among the racks in the boat area. If he wanted recognition for his achievements, it had to be given in a dignified and implicit way. I don't think he underestimated his contribution to our success. He wasn't a modest man. But people who forced their way into the foreground showed that they were insecure. And Schneiderhahn adopted an attitude that suggested he had expected all along that we should win race after race, as though it were an inevitable result of his approach, his schedules and his plans. Of course that simply increased his standing still further. He didn't require social intercourse for that.

Nevertheless I occasionally noticed his satisfaction. From a benevolent smile which appeared on his ruddy face at a moment when there was no immediate reason for it. From the cigar which he lit up and, triumphantly, made bob up and down between his teeth when, towards the end of a race day, he stood close to the stand and let his eyes wander over the jostling along the banks and round the finish.

It was the custom not to train the day after the race, and our coach ignored that custom too. We were supposed to report at the usual time, put the boat together and take to the water. I suspect that it was interpreted by outsiders as just one more proof of the eccentric and in fact rather inhuman training methods of Doktor Schneiderhahn. Though we might score successes, the way in which we did so wasn't really in keeping with an honest pursuit of our sport. Of course people didn't want to go that far in public, but in their minds they probably occasionally used the word 'unsporting'. Ultimately it wasn't just about medals but about . . . something that was part of the club and couldn't be explained to those who didn't understand.

People need not have worried in the least about those Monday training sessions after a race. Our instructions were to do exactly what we felt like, to make an effort or none at all: it was the only day we didn't have to follow a schedule. The intention was that we should 'actively' relax our tired muscles. Passive relaxation, Schneiderhahn explained to us, didn't exist. Both the body and the mind recover from one movement by executing another, in the same or a different fashion. On those Mondays without a programme we could do what we liked, enjoy the weather, the water, the memory of the day before, and we rowed in a disconcerting but not unpleasant vacuum. No *Fahrtspiel*, just rowing for pleasure. On those days Schneiderhahn stayed away and didn't cycle along to monitor our progress. We just rowed along for a bit, at first with muscles deliberately kept loose, silently giggling, with a little too much splashing.

Then we did a couple of starts, to get rid of the energy which was obviously still in us. They never went better than on those days after the race: the half, the full, the three-quarter and again full strokes. Fierce, blisteringly fast, regular as clockwork and carefree.

We rowed past the club, into town, and looked at the unfamiliar décor along this stretch of the river bank. We drifted, in the boat and in our thoughts. There was a large hotel not much further into town than the boathouse. It was painted white and thrust its balconies proudly out over the water. The lowest terraces stood proprietorially up to their knees in the river. We rowed past lazily. I felt an odd movement in the boat. When I looked round I saw that David had lain down, one arm outstretched and still gripping the oar, but with his body leaning back, his head almost resting on the waxed front canvas.

'Come on,' he grinned. 'Lie back. We'll ring and get the wine waiter to bring us a nice glass of beer!'

Cautiously I let my body lean back too, pulled my legs together but inevitably ended up with my head on David's outstretched shins. If I were to turn it even a little, my cheek would touch the hairs on his skin. I could feel him breathing, I could smell him. Just underneath me the water of the river moved very gently. If anyone had looked down from a first-floor balcony of the grand hotel, he would have seen two tanned lads lying as extensions of one another, the head of one not far from his friend's lap, tightly enclosed by the skin of their narrow boat, kept in balance by two thin oars. Motionless, surrounded by blue water, not a ship with a crew but a sarcophagus.

No one looked down. We looked up past the wide house fronts at the sky, which was almost as blue as the water. Perhaps swaying to and fro in just the same way. For a moment I lost the sense of what was up and what was down.

'Stately,' said David.

'Stately and vicious,' flashed through my mind. Like the swans floating in front of the terrace. And at the same moment the feeling of floating between the sky and the water had disappeared. I suddenly couldn't help thinking of everything that lay behind that immaculate front, of the kitchens and toilets, the shower cubicles and the sagging bodies of the people who used them, of the mortar, the lead, the deposits, the wood that was beginning to go soft at the ends, the brown rings and green mildew on the stucco work, men and women as bags of intestines. That whole tower of perishable materials erected on the bank, which perhaps dumped its rubbish in the river and whose foundations rested in the mud. It could easily collapse at any moment, and until that moment would go on silently rotting for every second that God gave. Everything that existed was destined to decay and I knew for certain that I wanted no part of that decay. Not ever. I belonged to the river. I mustn't get any older and it must stay forever summer. I sat up with a jerk, stretched my arms and said, 'Ready to row.' Without waiting to see whether David was actually ready to follow me, I rowed off. The boat moved off smoothly and effortlessly.

No movement without effort. No happiness without its accompanying pain, which you can feel, can point to, can grab by its thrashing tail when it would be easier to make no effort and allow it to slip away. More peaceful.

The sun shone every day. The training sessions became harder. The more we adjusted to each other, the more Schneiderhahn put the emphasis on shifting the pain barrier. We knew the creeping tiredness that came from covering a long stretch with firm strokes. We also knew the exertion required for a last pull of the dumbbells, the last ten strokes in a series. That took an effort, but still didn't really hurt. To experience real pain, you also have to overload your lungs.

Oxygen debt. Something has gone awry between you and the rest of the world, you need more air but you can't get any. You feel the pain not only in your chest, but mainly in the muscles which cause the debt. After twenty starting strokes, your arms and legs scream for more rest, less effort, a different tempo. Your thighs feel like enormous pistons, swelling up and threatening to burst out of their casing, balloons blown up to their full extent that threaten to explode at the next breath. Your biceps and forearms are stretched, as if someone has hung a weight on them – once more, and that's it, they know that for sure, and you can't pull them up to your chest. Your head goes on giving commands, louder and louder, but perhaps against its better judgement; it doesn't know whether the engine room can obey them, even if they are understood. What if the valves give out? Screams of protest. Have they gone crazy up there on the bridge?

Schneiderhahn made us row hard strokes in series which were intended to push up the oxygen debt. The interval between one series and the next was not quite long enough to replenish the supply. Before we were fully recovered we started on the next series.

It was not only pain but the fear of pain which shot through us each time just before we started the build-up to maximum effort. Pain and fear that alternated until they started to form a single rhythm and flow into each other. Was fear also part of happiness? It was almost bound to be. Fear and pain. The same intoxication.

And strategies for combating it.

In my mind I sorted the hard strokes into columns and sections. At lightning speed, I entered lines and numbers in my ledger; as I experienced it, I tried to alleviate reality by turning it into an abstraction. Or I tried to make a thing of our task, imagining that it consisted of objects that didn't hurt, but were simply there. You could store them away. I arranged them into boxes, compartments and shelves. Twenty deep breaths means five pigeonholes with four containers full of air. Or four piles of five stones that I have to put down. Not only does such a quantity of work mount up, what remains fortunately becomes less and less. Sprinting for thirty strokes? After the fifteenth, you're going downhill again. You cling to that idea.

But there was also the voice of Schneiderhahn, who in the middle of an explosion of power cried for discipline, control. Head *hoch*, Anton! David, steer! We had waves against us, fishermen on the bank who had cast too far out, a vague notion of weather and wind, mainly sun and heat, heat around us and heat inside, landmarks, a gate, a farm on the bank, scores of minor events to distract you. We were not just a machine trying to increase its power. There was also a boat which had to be kept in equilibrium and on course, and that boat, with its movement and its life, we were that too. I sometimes felt David trembling in my own arms and legs. I was fighting not only the water and the wind, but him too. I couldn't allow him to go on rowing harder and longer than me.

Whenever he put in more power, the boat would veer off course and slowly steer into the shore. My fault. But he was responsible for the course. So it was his too. Perhaps he sometimes contained himself so he still had extra energy when he adjusted his stroke to mine. The only way of reducing that risk was always to try as hard as possible to do my best, never to relax. That would force him to do the same. Ultimately, rowing hard, biting back the pain, were things I did not for the stopwatch of Schneiderhahn with his bike – the white hair and the white tyres behind the reeds. I did it for David, so as not to feel ashamed in front of him.

So were we still not equal? No. We were dissimilar in every way and he seemed to be superior in everything. Even my place as stroke, the one who determined the rhythm, I did not see as proof of my qualities. I felt that I had gained that place because I was less able than David to adjust to someone else, because I was not cool-headed enough to manoeuvre the rudder, because I constantly accelerated and slowed down during a race so that the rhythm was occasionally disrupted, a quality that was inextricably bound up with my character, with my stubborn form of perseverance, which had less to do with the will to win than with the fear of losing, of one day losing everything we had won so far. David had no problem with rowing bow. He corrected, he supported, he followed and, because of that, he was superior.

But one day we were standing on the landing stage in front of the boathouse and Schneiderhahn was laying down the law to us more sternly than usual about a training session which hadn't gone according to his wishes. The hundred-metre times had an arbitrary character that day, as if our tiredness had been full of unpredictable peaks and troughs. As if we'd only done our job half-heartedly.

'But we're both doing our best,' said David, defending himself.

'We're both rowing as hard as each other,' I supported him.

'*Unsinn!*' said Schneiderhahn. 'The stroke produces fifteen per cent more power. That's been scientifically proven.'

He turned on his heel and strode off. End of discussion.

In the changing-room we tried to reason out Schneiderhahn's thesis. David came up with the following theory. Because the rower in bow position is closer to the end of the boat in the direction it was moving, it is less effort for him to pull round the bow and change course. The man in the front constantly has to compensate by producing slightly more power.

Henceforth I would be able to include that factor in our calculations. When we were rowing home tired after the bridge, I could tell myself that I had filled more boxes and piled more stones than David. A strange feeling that I didn't quite know how to handle and that I therefore tried to put out of my mind.

I preferred to think about other things on that last stretch on the way home. For example, of the expression 'a thousand lakes'.

'Finland is the land of a thousand lakes,' David had once said.

And although our part of the Games might take place on a canal or at any rate on a manageable quantity of water close to the capital, when I thought of Finland I still thought automatically of a thousand lakes. A thousand wasn't a number. It cannot be quickly and neatly broken up into manageable pieces. A thousand is infinite. And as we covered the last few hundred metres to the jetty without instructions, tired and drained but usually also content, in my imagination I often rowed over the mirror of a calm lake whose shores could not be seen and which, behind us without our realizing, would merge into the next, and the next. There was no end to them, we could go on rowing without time and without counting and without getting tired because beyond every horizon there was another lake with another horizon. The sun, in Finland, would also shine for ever.

Schneiderhahn had talked to the club's committee. I tried to imagine how he had been received. With respect and extra politeness, because of his great experience as a coach, on the basis of our achievements and because he was in addition a foreigner, a guest?

I feared not. More probably his request had been listened to with an affability bordering on contempt. 'That's not the custom here, Mr Snyderhun, although you of course can't be expected to know that. Perhaps things are different in your country, but we'd rather not go into that.'

That's how they had sat opposite each other. The president of the club, who was finally able to present his limitations as a merit so that the Doktor could be taken down a peg or two. And the formidable Schneiderhahn, in his outlandish suit with the outsize checks and with his bristly head of hair, who had to do his best to hide his irritation and not to get angry because he had a request that only these *petit bourgeois* people could grant. Because he was a hotel resident and dependent on them.

Petit bourgeois? Did I already think like that about the self-important ladies and gentlemen of the club? No, I was still full of respect that summer, when I thought of them, the people I couldn't become one of, and at that moment perhaps already no longer wanted to be one of. The realization of their smallness only came with the years. In those years, Schneiderhahn has only increased in stature for me.

Of course it's also quite possible that our coach wasn't at all irritated, in the committee room with its green baize and its trophies and prints, but regarded the conversation as no more than a tiresome chore. Schneiderhahn had faced harder struggles, out there in his own country and in the south.

Whatever the case, he achieved the desired result. Our last race of that season was to be a special one. We were to row for the championship.

'A second-year crew?' said David, with raised eyebrows, and then he started laughing. I laughed with him. I felt frightened and proud at the same time. Where was Schneiderhahn taking us? Was the river no longer enough, then? Weren't our training sessions hard enough? How would we row on the thousand lakes?

Now it was Schneiderhahn's turn to raise his eyebrows. 'No reason to laugh, *meine Herren*. Results and age are two categories which intersect but don't overlap.'

He tapped his briefcase. Our training schedules were inside. And other papers. 'I've compared your results with the times of your possible opponents. In the course of the season those differences have become systematically smaller.'

With his fleshy hand, he now described an arc that rose above eye level. 'I can see from the training work that your curve is going up and up. Meanwhile' – a sudden, horizontal skimming movement with the same hand – 'the performance of the others has flattened out. They're not making any more progress.' Finally, an indulgent gesture with both arms. 'No plans, no progression.'

Disbelief had still not disappeared from David's face and the smile was still playing around his lips. 'So you think we're stronger than . . .' And he mentioned the names of well-known men, champions.

'Not yet,' answered Schneiderhahn. 'But we've still got three weeks. In my language there's a proverb that says, "Nothing ventured, nothing gained."'

'We've got that proverb in Dutch too,' retorted David.

We'd won so many times now. Eight times? Ten? I forget. I'd put the first few medals on the windowsill at home. But it was small and narrow. When more came, I had to move them to the ledge above the foldaway bed. They attracted less attention there and I liked that. Occasionally I picked them up and let them run through my hands, the bronze and metal discs with the self-important illustrations, coats of arms and symbols, and the date on which they'd been awarded. There was one with a red ribbon attached.

You'd think that every medal would bring back the

memory of an important event. But they weren't souvenirs. They had no meaning, they brought nothing to life. At most, they marked an event that had gone, been left behind, vanished for good. Only the moment of winning counted. And that moment was wonderful and unrepeatable. At most, it left behind emptiness, nothing tangible, not the medal but its impression.

In the course of each race my attention shifted, I noticed, in four stages, four steps to happiness.

During the start I was completely preoccupied with myself, concentrating, sometimes on the verge of panic, sometimes beyond it, trying to get the whole complicated machinery of boat and body into motion as quickly as possible.

When that had been successfully achieved and I had forced myself to keep my thoughts on the steady churning of our oars for a while, I glanced to the side and assessed our position. I assessed the pace and strength of our competitors, sometimes deciding on an intermediate sprint with a brief command, tried to reduce the oxygen debt to a bearable threshold.

As we passed the first kilometre mark and it was clear that this time we again had a good chance of appearing on the ceremonial raft, I felt the pain creeping deeper into my body. Still a kilometre to go – and in that kilometre my thoughts and feelings transferred from my own body to that of David. I felt how he supported me as if I were acquiring extra muscles. I wondered whether he could keep it up and kept going because he did. Through the pain I began to enjoy myself again and in the fourth and last stage, as we approached the finishing area and the sound of the oarsmen gave way to sounds from the bank, everything came together: my own body, David's, the speed of the boat, the opponents whom I now had completely in my sights because we were ahead of them – and the whole tangle of perceptions and feelings, which I could distinguish sharply from each other but which all affected me at once, together formed the feeling of happiness of the last few metres which erupted in a whistle signal, a hooter or a cannon shot. We'd won. And David, who with his first breath, as calmly as possible, said: 'Congratulations.' Had I made the effort for myself, for him, or for something beyond that? For the two of us?

I didn't know. I had put the medals away above the bed and was now standing in front of my little window. It had grown hot. The summer was to continue for ages, but the rowing season was now drawing to a close. I bent my head through the windowframe and tried to look into the street. Languid silence as far as Emerald Street. In my thoughts I turned the corner and reached the river. Why was I was not sad at the approach of the last race? Why didn't I feel apprehensive about the long months until September when I wouldn't see him and Schneiderhahn? My thoughts got no further than the water that now, in the summer evening, would be lying there talking to itself. Why was I so different from the year before?

I withdrew my head from the window and took two steps towards the mirror that had belonged to my grandfather. I took off my shirt and bent forward. In the mirror I could see only a small section of my body. The curve of my chest. A shoulder. My flat belly. Legs, hips. I sank to my knees, bent sideways, stretched, finally took the mirror off its hook and undressed completely to be able to look at myself all over in the light that came through the window. But in fact I didn't need a mirror. I stretched out, squeezed my arms, put my hands on my buttocks and pushed my chest and hips out. Everything I could see was terrific. With this body I could do anything. As I flexed all my muscles I knew that I'd never been so strong. That this summer there was no difference between alone and together. He was my mirror image and I was his. Through David, I'd come to love myself.

IV

Almost no lights are lit in the Eden Hotel these days. In fact, the paper on the panes no longer serves any purpose. There are no newspapers on the polished table in the lobby and no one sits in the plush armchairs waiting for someone. Everyone's waiting, but for no one in particular. The city is waiting, with its empty shop windows and its hollow people. Not because it has a date, but because it can't do much else but wait and think of the past. Under the window of my room, three floors below, is the canal. Black and dead as a cesspool, a stinking pond from which any instant poisonous bubbles can come bubbling up. You hope it will never start moving again, and it probably won't, it is too tired.

Only at the edges does it still lap spitefully at the houses, which are gradually being undermined by it. The process of decay and putrefaction has been going on for hundreds of years, it began when the first piles were driven into the mud and became saturated with moisture. But it wouldn't surprise me if this winter were to be the last, if the ulcer were now to burst and the whole terrace with all its memories of pleasure and sin were to topple forwards, slowly, in slow motion as in a modern film, vanishing into the depths and never floating to the surface again. The city goes under and submerges us in a dome of water. The river, curious, no longer keeps aloof. It overflows its banks, it ripples over the remains of roofs and walls, it washes away the exhaustion with it.

It's a miracle that I haven't been seen. Or perhaps it's not a miracle and the town, my town, is an ally tonight. I have packed my case. I have done little and hence not needed much here in the hotel in the last few months. A few clothes, starched and ironed, a cotton shirt that I haven't worn for five years. The blue books with the bell, black and gold, on the cover, exercise books with calculations. And two dumbbells, once red, now almost completely faded. I've closed the case and paid my bill.

Hurriedly, hugging the fronts of the buildings, I walked to the end of the narrow street. Behind me a last sight of the unlit sign of my hotel. Past the stock exchange, turning again into an alley, avoiding the main thoroughfares, I moved towards the river. Curfew. No one in the street. But mounds of rubbish on every corner, because it was no longer being collected. Near the market I went down a small set of steps to let the case slip into the water. It stayed afloat for a moment, astonished and unfamiliar with its destination, and then the dumbbells did their final work. Not even a ripple remained on the surface.

Now I had two hands to hold my coat shut. The cold bit into my fingers and pierced beneath my collar. It drove all the smells from the air, as though able to prevent not only happiness but decay, as if those two were the same, as though able to stop everything. Even when I approached the river, I could still not smell it. It suddenly loomed up in front of me. No moon. I could just make out the silhouette of a bridge. But I didn't cross yet. I kept walking in the shadow of the houses, with the water on my left, until I reached the new bridge, our bridge, the one with the electric lamps, which were removed long ago. The iron of the balustrade was a blazing strip of cold through the night. I touched it for a moment and had to withdraw my hand almost immediately. I slid from lamp to lamp in stages. I had never counted them. I was able to find the middle without difficulty. And because I had the feeling that nothing could happen to me any more, I stopped.

Water beneath me, moving restlessly, stretching and swaying as if it knew it was soon to freeze. Winter air that was armed with knives and needles and hurt my eyes. Somewhere to the left of me, our neighbourhood with its streets named after gems, with its paving stones that suggested waves but had never moved, ponderous and solid, without a past. These streets should be spared, together with my father and my mother, because they had no notion of decay. They were built on sand, not on water. The people lived there free of sin and yet I was glad that I no longer belonged there. I started moving again. It's easier downhill. I counted six lamps without lights. In the distance I knew I would find the derelict clubhouse.

The days preceding the championship were strange. Schneiderhahn had forbidden us to row hard, he even gave us three whole days off training. We had to feel hungry for the water, long for powerful strokes. I wandered through the town, aimless and content, but at the same time with a feverish excitement. The excitement was not just the usual kind, which consisted mainly of fear of pain. There was something else, connected with the shadow that a great event can cast ahead of it, with the feeling that perhaps we really were something special, that we would be able to achieve the impossible. That we would appear together in the papers, as champions, David and I.

A championship is something different from an ordinary victory. You don't own a championship like you own a medal. A champion is something that you are. It's not part of a moment but of a period. However old you become, whatever happens, wherever you are, even in the hour of your death: you will always have been a champion.

I wandered through the streets and along the canals, I jumped on a tram and let it take me past the markets and the shops. I looked at the dresses, the hats, the summer coats of the people, and saw that they had no bodies under their clothes. No bodies like mine, that could do anything.

If there was one message that was given to me by my parents, it was the conviction that we were nothing special and that we should not be distinguished in anything from our neighbours. There is a lot of truth in that thought. It's also a kind of consolation. I have no special talents, I can't do anything that someone else can't do just as well, and I don't feel any need to do so. There's nothing that I've ever wanted to achieve. But there was a summer when every- thing fell into my lap. I glided through the town as if in a dream, not knowing that a dream is at its most beautiful just before one wakes. I felt the material of my trousers sliding over my thighs, I felt my shoulders and my chest under my shirt. I felt a champion among men.

A strong wind was blowing across the Bosbaan course, making the flags flap viciously. The thousands of spindly trees which had been dispatched to form a wood shivered in the breeze. With their puny branches they bent towards each other, but they'd been planted at regular distances and were still too small to touch their neighbours. The martial music from the loudspeakers was also simply blown away, past our ears, up into the great sky. Harsh light fell over the new stand. The rowing course lay amid the open park land-scape like an alien slice of water, with brightly coloured buoys marking out the six lanes, and straight edges.

The course had been dug by the unemployed, who had also planted the wood. My father had occasionally talked about it. With contempt, under which he just managed to conceal the fear that he might have been there himself, early in the morning in his thickest clothes, while water bubbled up under his feet and seeped into his shoes, his muscles still aching from the previous day, and on his hands, his narrow hands, the blisters swelling under the insufficient layer of calluses and opening so that sticky liq-uid ran down his fingers, around which he wrapped a glove or a rag as he bent over again and dug the shovel into the muddy earth amid all those other painful backs around him. If he'd ever thought about it, he would have won-dered why those poor devils had to dig instead of build, make a place to accommodate the water instead of con-structing a street with roofs for themselves. But he didn't think about it. He simply thanked his lucky stars that he had escaped their fate. And he was right, he wouldn't have wanted to dig the course for me, and wouldn't have wanted to have the hands, my calloused oarsman's hands with bumps and flakes of skin that I was so proud of.

Schneiderhahn looked at the wind, the wind tugged at his jacket and at his short hair. We had drawn station six, the lane furthest from the finishing tower and the stand. There was thunder in the look with which Schneiderhahn observed the wind and the water. The three of us stood in the grass along the roadway opposite the stand and he pointed to the ducks which without exception swam to the other side, towards buoy one. Shelter. Schneiderhahn took a piece of paper out of his pocket and, bending over the saddle of his bike, folded it into a boat, in fact more of a pointed hat, with his fat fingers. He tried to throw it into the water but it didn't get very far. It landed close to the bank and yet far enough away to see that it moved backwards and forwards wildly on the waves and made scarcely any headway. 'In this wind the low-numbered buoys have an advantage,' growled Schneiderhahn. Then he pulled himself together. 'But we have the advantage of surprise and youth.'

A car stopped just behind us. We heard the door open and then a cultured voice greeting us cheerfully. We turned and Schneiderhahn shook hands with the president of the club, a tall man with hair combed straight back and gleaming with pomade. His car was a dark-red Delage with black mudguards and a white wall around the tyres and headlamps which protruded above the radiator. Something went on ticking under the hood for a moment and then the thing just stood there, gleaming with its elongated, restrained presence.

The president spoke about the rowing course. Hands on his back, sometimes with a single expansive gesture. As if he himself had commissioned the building and as if it had been just designed, and not also dug out spade by spade. He talked about the roomy, modern changing-rooms and the prospects for organizing the Games in our city again. He wished us luck. He scarcely resembled David at all, except for the smile around his thin mouth. A smile with which you could say everything and which at the same time made it clear that you were above it all. 'And if you two win I'll personally drive you home in triumph through the city . . .' Was that a serious announcement, a promise or a superior form of silence? Could you rely on something that was said to you in a tone like that? Or should you always allow for the possibility that there was something that you hadn't understood? I didn't have the knack, that smile. Nor did Schneiderhahn. He was brusque, almost curt with the president, who didn't seem to mind. Was it just the wind and our unfavourable draw that were weighing on Schneiderhahn? He looked pale today, almost grey, as grey as the water of the unfair course.

I wasn't afraid. Of course I hadn't slept the night before the race. In the spacious, modern toilet area, where there was an appalling stench even early in the day, my intestines had emptied as they did before every race. I had read the programme at least five times and learned the names of our opponents by heart. I was so tense that I forgot to be frightened and when we took to the water to row to the start the wind had died down too. So we had got worried for nothing.

Schneiderhahn worried, old Schneiderhahn had been through the race with us and given us yet another new piece of advice. It sounded like the last thing he had in his briefcase. Everything that he knew, we now knew too. From now on there weren't three of us but two, and that didn't feel like a problem. Out of the corner of my eye I could see that the stand was half full. I pushed the pace up a couple of times to get warm. The music sounded louder, the flags now flapped festively instead of anxiously. The boat reacted in a familiar way to our hard strokes, as though it were eager. You would have said that even the trees were rustling approval if they hadn't been too small for that. A little later we had reached the end of the rect-angle, had turned and were ready for the start.

On buoy one, with the luck of champions, were last year's title-holders, powerful young men in dark-blue vests with identical serious expressions under identical dark-blond curls. They could have been twins. Next to them, two crews in red, the two halves of a coxed four which – out of bravado, to decide which part of their team was really the strongest, in order to have an extra chance of a title – had entered for more than one event. Then on buoy four, two men I didn't know, their white shirts decorated on the back with a red star. David knew that they had already been champions more than once in the old four and in the eight, he knew their names, he knew the names of their fathers. They mastered all disciplines. Finally, next to us in lane five, a strange, ill-matched pair, a small, dark boy with hollow eyes and behind him a long, skinny chap with a quiff and a pockmarked face who seemed so large that he could have hidden his mate in the space between his knees and his chin. Van Groningen and Atsma, who for three years running had been champions in the coxed pair, and two years ago in the coxless pair as well. They were ugly, and wore ugly shirts, dull orange with a black, six-pointed star on the chest. The tall boy yawned incessantly.

Others channelled their nervousness into the tightening of the nuts on the stretcher or into gripping and releasing the handle of their oar. It had got warm. Summer without wind. In front of the starting tower lay six boys who held the sterns of the boats just behind the rudder, like fish, just behind the head. They shifted around on the orders of a man on the bank, backwards and forwards until the front tips were precisely in line. When that had happened, the umpire raised his white flag as a sign that the starting procedure could begin. But one of the red chaps put his hand up, his boat had gone askew. He rowed a couple of short, angry strokes, looked round again and nodded. The shifting could recommence.

I still wasn't frightened and yet the tension sent an electric wave right through my body. I could feel it relaxing and stiffening in turn. Still, my heart was pounding in my throat.

White flag. Red flag. The first command of the starter.

'Get ready to start.' And all the strength went out of me.

'Are you . . .' A noise from the furthest corner of the course. The champions had started too quickly. The tension had been too much for them. Next to us, other teams now also set off with a couple of lazy strokes at a very low rate, to get the nervousness out of their system. 'Let go,' I said to the boy, who immediately let us go. We rowed five or six strokes and I felt my strength returning. I had been through this before. A false start is a boon for someone with weak nerves. 'Please stay on your stations!' shouted the starter angrily.

Everything had to be repeated. But a small sliver had been taken from the despair, setting out was no longer unknown territory.

Get straight. White flag. Red flag. Hands still looking for the right place on the handle. Silence.

'Get ready . . .'

Again that stiff anxiety. The silence is so deep that it begins to hum. Piercing sun.

'Are you ready . . .'

The whole world is longing for sound. For the release of breath that has been held.

'Go!'

It is five hundred metres from the bridge with the empty lanterns to the front door of the club, to where the front door of the club used to be. How often have I walked that distance? I could have taken every step with my eyes closed. But now I really was almost blind, in this dark, freezing-cold night it turned out that I did not know the pathway. I was no longer walking close to the houses, where the pavement is wide and light, but along a small and narrow footpath by the edge of the water that had been made uneven by time, rain and the roots of trees. Once I stumbled, but with a hand in the wet grass was able to stand up again. The paving stones overlapped like ice floes. They wobbled, or I wobbled and they moved with me. The water next to me made no sound. The tall houses on the other side looked down pityingly at me. I imagined that their letter-boxes were pressed shut like disdainful lips.

Close to the club, the pavement had disappeared entirely, having gone with the demolition. I felt sand under my feet. I stopped and looked up. Here the steps led up to the first floor, where the front door was, above the boathouse. Here I had walked beside my father one day in autumn. No, I walked ahead of him. I forced him to go to the committee room behind me. Up. I shook him off me. I took a lead that I never again surrendered.

'Go!' The red flag is dropped. The first strokes after the start are a release. Three-quarters. Half. Half. Three-quarters. Full. Dipping sharply, bouncing in the waves, the boat gathers speed. Splashing water. Sunlit. My shoulders and my knees do the work. I'm particularly pleased with the two half-strokes, they catch viciously, my heart leaps. In the transition to the thirty hard starting strokes, the boat first moves unwillingly as though it has something to shake off, tipping to starboard side, falling over to port side, but then it catches. We shoot away, still accelerating, and without being aware of it I've started counting. As early as stroke twenty, where the first pain starts, I look to the side for the first time. The field is still bunched together, only the old chaps with the red star are a little behind. Spluttering, the motorboat with the umpire on board leaves the bank, in order to sail to the middle of the course. There it will soon follow us, a man is standing upright with a flag in his hand and wearing a blue blazer, despite the heat, to check that no one leaves their lane. I have almost no problem with my oxygen debt. After thirty strokes I let the strike rate gradually drop to find a balance between power and endurance. When I succeed in doing that, I dare to look to the side for a little longer. Next to us the ugly lads are rowing. My blade shaves past the orange-coloured blade of the tall chap with the quiff, scarcely two metres away. But David keeps us right in the middle of our lane. I have a good feeling, as though it is not I, the boy of just now, from before the start, that is pulling his oar across through the water, but a better, stronger person who has been trained for this work. We're away. It's begun. All decisions have been made. Rhythm. Head up. Controlled breathing. Along the bank a procession of cyclists is moving. Over the course a steel wire with a numbered board hangs above every lane. It gives the distance. Five hundred metres. A quarter of the race is over.

The stairs are no longer there, but in my imagination I still see them ascending to the double doors with their decoration of wooden waves. The brass knob. Behind it, the corridor with the door to the changing-room. Rough wooden benches, which have been wetted a thousand times and dried again. A discarded shirt, dirty, swept into a corner. A lump of cracked soap. Steam leaking through the narrow windows. A memory hangs in the air, a memory with floors and walls, the memory of the first floor which hasn't existed for a number of days. In reality, nothing is left. Not even any smells. Even the gate next to the boathouse that gives access to the landing stage has been half-demolished.

Barbed wire has been strung carelessly across the opening. I bent it aside with my hands. My fingers were grazed and scratched, and began bleeding. Because of the cold, I only felt the pain after I saw it. I pulled a plank out of the temporary gate, which snapped off loudly in the silence. I didn't even take the trouble to wait and see if anyone had heard and had come towards me, so sure was I that I would be left alone tonight. Houses can be alone, I thought as I wriggled my way through the gap in the gate. Boats need people. There are no boats left. The shed is empty. Tomorrow, or else the day after tomorrow, the last piece of the building will have been demolished. It's a thought that floats free in the air, it's a memory that has lost almost all of its substance

The stretch between five hundred and a thousand metres is the dullest in any race. The important thing is to find a rowing rhythm that you can keep up, not easily but close to your limit, and then to stay in that groove. Three-quarters of the distance is still ahead of you. It is still too early to waste lots of energy on an acceleration or an intermediate sprint. And even a teasing surge can be difficult – can you regain your rhythm afterwards? Most races are decided in the second five hundred metres.

I felt the sweat running into my neck and down my back, and on my forearms too, which I saw stretching in front of me, there was a film of liquid. My breathing pounded regularly. I could think. So this was it. The last race of the season, a race which six months ago we wouldn't have dared to dream of. And now we were in the middle of it, in the stadium where the contenders were separated from the losers. The short and the tall man were still rowing alongside us, remarkably smoothly. They had even gained a slight lead on us, but I wasn't worrying about that yet. On the far side the title-holders hadn't completely disappeared from my field of vision, a good sign. The old men had fought their way back; after a cautious start, in a type of boat they didn't know through and through, but with reserves of routine that they now drew on. Only the two red crews were scarcely in contention, and were losing ground visibly with every stroke. They were probably already arguing with each other, if not in words then through the clumsy movements with which the oarsmen were working against each other. Another hundred metres perhaps and they would have lost touch with the field and they would see only each other, would hear the sound of the other boats becoming fainter and fainter behind their backs and know there was nothing left for them in this race.

There was for us. While I thought – simple thoughts, driven directly by my arms and legs – I suddenly realized that the others were looking at me too and were undoubtedly thinking the same kinds of things. They weren't the field, *we* were. Without the red guys now.

We were still part of it. I glanced to the side again and could just see the small orange guy looking at me. With his mouth wide open he resembled a bird gasping for breath. His strike rate was higher than mine. The old men were both actually looking, their experience compensating for their lack of discipline. Were the crew next to us and the men on buoy one increasing their lead over us? Were the white shirts with the red star closing on us? Next to me I saw the puddles suddenly getting larger, a sign that they'd started an intermediate sprint. Above our heads the thousand-metre board flew past. I said 'Yes', too softly perhaps, and picked up the pace for twenty hard strokes. Past halfway. Downhill now, but still harder. Whether David had heard me I don't know, but he understood me equally well without words. We accelerated.

I forced my way between lumps of concrete from which the iron protruded with deformed claws, past beams and posts. My feet shuffled through the unrecognizable rubble that remains when the major connecting structures are demolished, the grit of paving stones, tiles, shards, the dust of wasted years. Occasionally my foot struck something that crackled, or gave way; cardboard or paper, sediment from the vanished rooms, an archive that wasn't worth rescuing. Demolition is like moving house and we never take everything with us when we move.

I didn't enter the boathouse, although a door was open and I could have. I had no illusions about what I would find there. But I did stop for a moment and I found myself listening to see if anything was happening inside, half expecting to hear the sound of dumbbells being lifted and put down. Then I began walking along the jetty, which was very slippery, pitch black and slippery, and which already had planks missing from it. I had to concentrate on every step, arms outstretched, fingers bleeding, my coat wide open. But every step was one more in the direction of the water.

After the sprint strokes, I had continued counting. Counting down: hundreds of metres, strokes, parts of strokes, the catch and the finish. I had to divide the work into portions, a sign that exhaustion in its full magnitude had now come between us. Pain was on board. And I couldn't judge properly whether the intermediate sprint had helped. Again we were alongside the team with the orange blades, but had our sprint just made up for theirs or had we really caught up a little? Yes, we'd gained a little; the men in white, one of whom was already a little bald, had not closed the gap and now seemed to be falling back further, as their strike rate went down. But the bird-head's blade was now catching very close to mine. I looked at our stern and saw the rudder thrusting aside a wave. Was David pulling me off course then? Weren't we going straight any more? He corrected, not with the oars but with his foot. I tried to step up the power without changing rhythm, but unintentionally moved forwards a little faster on my seat.

The chugging of the umpire's boat, which seemed to be dying away slowly at first, rose abruptly in tone and in volume. The man in the blazer had decided not to keep behind the two red teams any longer. They were too far behind the other four. The bow wave of the boat disrupted any last trace of coherence they might have had as he lifted first one and then the other and swept them aside, out of the race.

'Look out!' shouted a furious David. Not at me, but at the boat next to us. The orange boat had come perilously close to ours. It wasn't David, able to produce more power than myself, it was the tall lad who was being dragged off course by the bird, his stroke. I almost struck his blade with mine. I looked to the side and saw panic in his eyes, and I enjoyed it. He could no longer avoid the following buoy, orange hit red, a hateful sound. For a moment their boat was askew in the lane, they missed a stroke and after that needed five or six to regain their rhythm. 'Yes,' I said, and while I prepared for a new intermediate sprint it was as if I felt myself creaking. Fifteen hundred metres. Five hundred to go. On the other side I could no longer see the blue shirts of the title-holders. Where were they? They had crept away into the lee as they approached the finish line.

Before I reach the water I turn round once more towards the clubhouse and see a second staircase that has disappeared. It led up from the raft to the terrace and to the changing-rooms. It is the staircase that I sometimes found it difficult to climb after a heavy training session. It is the staircase on which I saw Schneiderhahn for the last time, the day after our last race, the one for the championship.

The fact that even after that race we were expected to report on the raft on Monday afternoon made me glow with joy. So nothing was over, not even for a few months; we were going on, the summer would go on.

Schneiderhahn was waiting for us, without a briefcase, with the careworn expression which had characterized him for days, but also with something like relief, as if after taking a difficult, unpleasant decision. He spoke to us, not after, but before the training session. He was going away again. Where to, he didn't say, not even a direction was revealed to us. I expected him to give us new papers, just as he had that afternoon a year before, but he was empty-handed and he didn't have his case with him and in fact he didn't say that much. He urged us not to forget anything and I think I understood at once that he wasn't just talking about the schedules.

As we pushed off from the raft, he turned and walked up the steps, but while we rowed the first strokes and felt how tired and painful our bodies still were, I looked up and saw that he'd stopped half-way between the water and the ter-race, with his bristly hair, fleshy face, brown checked suit and under it, despite the heat, his calf-length shoes on the steel steps. We set off and soon he was just a silhouette with slightly rounded forms against the white background of the clubhouse. He raised his hand. That's the last we ever saw of Doktor Alfred Schneiderhahn. And now not even the steps are there any more.

I turn round and see only the black water.

The sound from the stands swelled – cheers, chanting, snatches of music – but the twins in the dark-blue shirts had disappeared. How far ahead they were was impossible to say. I couldn't look over my shoulder, hearing anything was impossible, and apart from that we now had to devote all our attention to ourselves. There was no question any longer of an intermediate sprint, it was now a matter of raising the strike rate and the power with every stroke. With each stroke we braced ourselves against the barrier of water, but also against our own limits. My hands were

hooked around the handles of the oars, I could feel my forearms gradually becoming hard and stiffening. My legs and
arms pumped with the last remnants of energy and my
back seemed to be made of elastic stretched to breaking
point. But while each of us was groaning to himself,
together we were fantastic. The boat flew forward, every
stroke was made by a single, possessed oarsman. We'd
made it. We couldn't row better together. A memory, really
more of a feeling, flashed through me and took me back to
an afternoon long ago when we had rowed in the rain. It
wasn't as effortless now, but it did go as naturally. And
much, much faster.

Even before we got to the stand I saw the dark-blue
shirts again level with us. Atsma and Van Groningen had
left their lane next to us, but that didn't matter, they were
behind us and only disadvantaged themselves by the hindrance they experienced from our wake. However, the old
men had found something in themselves, or perhaps
they'd managed to save it up for this moment, and now ral-
lied with surprising speed. With every swishing stroke
they made, I saw the red star on their backs coming closer.
Their bow was now level with our rudder, five strokes later
the man in the bow was almost alongside. So the six of us,
no, the three of us, shot along in three boats with six men,
over the last two hundred and fifty metres to the finish.

Schneiderhahn had given his final advice cautiously and
only on the morning of this last race day. It wasn't the intention that we should follow it, we had to cherish it and derive
self-confidence from it, it was a secret weapon that we'd do
better not to use. 'When you see the first row of flagpoles in

front of the stand,' he had announced solemnly, 'there are precisely eleven strokes left to the finish. If you are sure that nothing else will help, if the race will otherwise be lost, you can decide to sprint flat out at that point.'

The flat-out sprint is different from the final sprint. That's always at maximum, but also according to the rules; the tempo goes up with the power. In a flat-out sprint all rules are put aside, they are cancelled out, it takes place in no man's land. Only the rate counts, you must only think of that, you increase it in the hope that your body will cooperate and will derive from its memory the force that it doesn't actually have and forget itself instead of collapsing. Because that's the risk, that everything will collapse, like a building from which one post has been pulled. 'If it goes well, then the building will stay upright, a miracle will happen. But the most important thing that you must know about the flat-out sprint is this: don't do it. Try not to need it.'

I looked to the side again and saw the first flagpole. 'Flat out,' said David.

Eleven strokes. I shot forward and threw my shoulders and arms across my knees, pulled, followed through, wasn't even aware of my blade leaving the water, shot forward again like a catapult behind my hands – and David followed. I don't know if we went any faster, but I know it felt faster; the movement that we fell into, that we created, felt like pure speed itself.

Ten. Nine. The cheering from the stands swelled to a tunnel of sound into which we were sucked and in which one sound was no longer distinguishable from the next.

Eight. Seven. Images too merge into each other, the flags,

the people, the spokes in the president's car become strips and flashes indistinguishable from sound.

Six. Five. In the final stage it's everyone for himself, you're alone. Our opponents have disappeared. Next will be David.

Four. Three. And then myself.

Two. Of the stories that David told me, the riddle of Achilles and the tortoise, of the arrow speeding towards its target, has also remained with me. Achilles can't beat the tortoise and the arrow never hits the bull's-eye, however fast it goes, because it always has to go half, a smaller and smaller half of the remaining distance. Is he moving or standing still? That's how the final strokes before the finish felt; as if the last stroke would never come. As if there were no longer any difference between sound and silence, light and dark, movement and stasis, pain and deliverance, as though we had already won and had yet to become champions. At the top of the wave the water turns to ice.

Water becomes ice. Ice can become water again. The water is inky black, it laps at my feet. It is as black as the windows of David's big house, the house on the park that is now empty and from which all life has disappeared. The water starts to move and washes across the wood of the jetty like a wafer-thin membrane. I lie flat on my back and the water is sucked up by my coat. I lie back and look up to where it is just as black as it is around me.

When the planes return from the east tomorrow, the weary airmen will see from their cockpits the day breaking and the light moving with them from east to west across the wretched countryside. They will see the first shafts of sun-light lighting up certain spots with silver. A lake, a pond, a canal, a stretch of river that embraces the curve of our city like a child's arm. And as night turns to day, everything becomes double on the water, a tree bends over and sees itself mirrored, as do the birds, the clouds, a boat, a fisher-man, Anton and David. Pairs created by the water, the only liberation that means anything to me.

The cold has disappeared. The smells are returning. Cocoa floats over the water, a bitter-sweet aroma. No one can convince me that you can't touch happiness, that there is such a thing as happiness without a body. I close my eyes. Right through my drenched clothes I can feel the warmth of summer.

I open my eyes, look up and see David standing behind me. His sturdy legs, with the thick black hair. I hear his voice. He is trying to help me to my feet, but I get up by myself. Then we walk together in the direction of the clubhouse, the stairs are there again, and he puts an arm round my shoulder. The sun shines as if it will never stop. We're champions without having won.

'Better luck next year. Next year in Finland, Anton.'

And I think: a thousand lakes.

But I say: 'So you're not going away, we'll go on rowing.'

'Yes.'

'Say it. Say it in words.'

'We'll go on rowing. That's a promise.'